There was a naked body in the bed! A naked *male* body.

"What the hell—" said a furious voice.

Josie tried to say something, but couldn't. Her heart was thumping so fast that it was making her feel quite breathless.

A couple of moments later, there was a click of a switch, and a lamp beside the bed came on. Josie found herself staring straight into the face of a man who looked very, *very* angry. On the other hand, she wasn't feeling too even-tempered herself.

"What are you doing in my bed?" she demanded fiercely, finding her voice again as her erratic heartbeat began to slow down just a little.

"This happens to be *my* bed," came his terse reply. Then his gaze swept over her, taking in her state of undress. "And I don't remember ordering anything from room service," he added very coldly.

JOANNA MANSELL finds writing hard work but very addictive. When she's not bashing away at her typewriter, she's usually got her nose buried in a book. She also loves gardening and daydreaming, two pastimes that go together remarkably well. The ambition of this Essex-born author is to write books that people will enjoy reading.

Books by Joanna Mansell

HARLEQUIN PRESENTS
1291—THE SEDUCTION OF SARA
1331—A KISS BY CANDLELIGHT
1364—DEVIL IN PARADISE
1394—EGYPTIAN NIGHTS
1436—HAUNTED SUMMER
1482—PAST SECRETS

HARLEQUIN ROMANCE
2836—THE NIGHT IS DARK
2866—SLEEPING TIGER
2894—BLACK DIAMOND

JOANNA MANSELL

Land of Dragons

Harlequin Books

TORONTO • NEW YORK • LONDON
AMSTERDAM • PARIS • SYDNEY • HAMBURG
STOCKHOLM • ATHENS • TOKYO • MILAN
MADRID • WARSAW • BUDAPEST • AUCKLAND

Harlequin Presents first edition January 1993
ISBN 0-373-11523-7

Original hardcover edition published in 1991
by Mills & Boon Limited

LAND OF DRAGONS

Printed in U.S.A.

CHAPTER ONE

JOSIE crawled off the plane at Dum Dum airport outside Calcutta, and felt as if she had been travelling forever. All she wanted right now was to tumble into a soft bed and sleep for at least a week. Then the hot, humid air hit her, and she wilted still further. Her holiday hadn't even begun properly yet, and she already felt a total wreck!

There was a coach waiting to take the passengers from the plane to their hotel. Nearly all of them were tourists, booked on various package tours. Some were travelling around northern India, a few were staying in Calcutta for a couple of days before moving on to Kathmandu, in Nepal, and just a handful, like her, were going to a small country that was even more remote.

Although she had been on the plane with them for so many hours, Josie hadn't got beyond exchanging a few smiles and pleasantries with her fellow passengers. She supposed it was because everyone else was travelling either in pairs or groups. She was the only one mad enough to have come all this way on her own.

Of course, *she* should have had someone with her, she reminded herself resentfully. A fierce anger flashed in her dark blue eyes, intensifying their colour still further. She made an effort to get it under control, but only partly succeeded. Her nerves were still too raw, her anger too fresh and sharp to be easily pushed into the background.

She was still scowling as she clambered tiredly into the coach. There was an empty seat beside her, as there had been on the plane. Although it was a nagging reminder of the turmoil and upsets of the last couple of weeks, she was also perversely pleased that it was empty. It meant that they hadn't been able to sell Derek's ticket, and he would have to pay for it. Good! she thought with a swift rush of satisfaction. That was one of the penalties you paid for cancelling at the last moment!

It was a very hollow sense of satisfaction that she was feeling, though. And after a while that empty seat just kept reminding her that she was totally on her own. That made her feel uncomfortably nervous. She had travelled on her own before, but never this far, or to a land that seemed quite so foreign.

It had been crazy to come by herself, of course. She had told herself that a hundred times—but she had still marched determinedly on to the plane back in London. She was well aware that it had been little more than an act of defiance—and one that she was already regretting—but she was here now, in India. There was little she could do except grit her teeth and pretend like mad that she was enjoying every minute of it.

Josie looked out of the window, at waterlogged fields with buffaloes plodding stoically through the muddy water. It was the monsoon season—not a good time to come to this part of the world. Then the coach rattled into the city itself, and Josie got her first look at Calcutta.

She had read somewhere that someone had once described it as a hell on earth. And if you didn't like crowds, you would probably agree with that! she thought to herself. Calcutta was certainly incredibly overcrowded. The roads and pavements were packed with people. They seemed to live, eat, sleep, wash themselves and their clothes, and sell everything under the sun right there, on the streets. Herds of goats and cows jostled for space with the teeming traffic, and there were some *very* strange smells wafting in through the coach windows. Rickshaws, lorries and cars wove their way through the packed streets with reckless abandon, horns blared continuously, pedestrians and animals seemed to move out of the way at the very last moment and somehow, miraculously, no one was killed or even hurt.

To Josie's relief, it didn't take them too long to reach their hotel. At any other time, she would probably have thought Calcutta was noisy, smelly, exotic, exciting and bustling, but she really didn't feel up to coping with it right now!

She stumbled into the hotel, almost asleep on her feet. After scrawling her name in the registration book, she grabbed the key the clerk handed her, glanced at the number, and headed towards the stairs.

She was on the first floor, room fifteen. Yawning hard, she fumbled with the key as she reached the room, but then found that she didn't need it. The door was already unlocked.

Inside, the room was very dark since the shutters were closed. Josie didn't bother to open them. She could just make out the dim outline of the bed, and that was all she needed to see for now. With a sigh of relief, she kicked off her shoes, wriggled out of her

thin cotton jeans and T-shirt, but couldn't be bothered
to take off her bra and pants. Giving another huge
yawn, she padded towards the bed. She knew she
ought to shower, ought to unpack, ought to have
something to eat. She was just too tired, though. More
than anything, she needed to sleep.

She groped for the bed, only just able to see it in
the darkness. There was a thin cover, which she pulled
back. Then she thankfully tumbled into it, her leaden
eyelids already drooping shut.

A split second later, though, she let out a loud yelp
of alarm. Then she tumbled right out of the bed again,
dragging the cover with her.

There was a naked body in the bed! A naked *male*
body. For just an instant, she had curled right up
against it.

'What the hell——?' said a furious voice.

Josie tried to say something, but couldn't. Her heart
was thumping so fast that it was making her feel quite
breathless.

A couple of moments later, there was the click of
a switch, and a lamp beside the bed came on. Josie
found herself staring straight into the face of a man
who looked very, *very* angry. On the other hand, she
wasn't feeling too even-tempered herself.

'What are you doing in my bed?' she demanded
fiercely, finding her voice again as her erratic heartbeat
began to slow down just a little.

'This happens to be my bed,' came his terse reply.
Then his gaze swept over her, taking in her state of
undress. 'And I don't remember ordering anything
from room service,' he added very coldly.

At that, Josie's dark blue eyes positively blazed.
She knew perfectly well that, in some hotels, in ex-

change for a large tip, a woman could be discreetly brought to a man's room. But to insinuate that *she* was here for that purpose...

She glowered fiercely at him. 'I shouldn't think any woman in her right mind would want to share your bed, even if you *did* offer to pay,' she flung at him insultingly. 'And if you don't get out of this room— my room—in five seconds flat, then I'm going to call the manager. In fact, I'll have you arrested. And I don't think you'll like the local gaols very much!'

The man slowly sat up, and Josie tried to keep glaring at him without actually looking at him, which wasn't particularly easy. If she looked away, it would be a sign of weakness on her part, and give him an advantage that she definitely didn't want him to have. On the other hand, the man was naked! Now that the first flush of fear and anger was past, it was difficult to look at him without a rather embarrassed blush creeping across her face.

In the end, she compromised by looking at a point just above his head. He, in turn, seemed to have no such qualms, and stared directly at her.

Josie pulled the sheet more closely round her. 'I don't like perverts,' she hissed at him. 'If you need to get your kicks by staring at women, find someone else to play your sick little games!'

His gaze hardened. 'And I don't like girls who creep into my bed, hoping to make some quick, easy money.'

'I did not creep into your bed,' Josie howled at him. 'This is *my* bed. I've got a key to this room, I've every right to be here. I wouldn't touch your money, or you!'

'But you already have,' he reminded her. His voice was a little smoother now, as if he was getting some control over his own temper. 'In fact, when I woke up, you were curled up right beside me.'

'Because I didn't know you were there! And I wish you'd put some clothes on,' she added edgily. 'You probably think that your body is quite wonderful, but I'm getting very tired of looking at it.'

'You've actually looked just about everywhere, except at my body,' he remarked, and there was almost a hint of amusement in his tone now. 'But if it bothers you that much——'

'It doesn't bother me at all,' she denied hotly at once, and completely untruthfully. To her intense relief, he pulled on a pair of jeans that had been tossed casually over the chair beside the bed.

'Don't *you* want to get dressed?' he said rather pointedly.

'Oh—yes,' Josie said very hurriedly. She dragged on her own jeans and T-shirt, and felt slightly better now that they were both fairly decent. At least, she was decent. He was still naked from the waist up, but she thought she could just about cope with that.

He sat on the edge of the bed and looked up at her. By the light of the lamp, she could see that his eyes were gold-brown. Tiger eyes, she thought irrelevantly. And his hair was the same colour, tousled gold-brown strands that were swept back from a high, strong forehead.

'Now that we seem to have stopped shouting at each other, perhaps we can get this cleared up,' he suggested.

'It's perfectly simple. You're in the wrong room,' she said firmly.

'I think that you're the one who's made the mistake.'

'Definitely not,' Josie said with a fresh rush of irritation. 'I've got the key to this room. How could I possibly have that, if I'd made a mistake?'

'Did you open the door with it?'

'No, the door was already unlocked.'

'That was because I had already unlocked it, with *my* key.'

'That's impossible,' Josie insisted.

'Where is your key?'

'Here, in my pocket,' she said, fishing it out of her jeans.

'Let me take a look at it.'

She tossed it over to him, and then stared at him defiantly. 'I'm right, aren't I? That's the key to room fifteen—my room.'

'No,' he said calmly. 'This is the key to room sixteen.'

'*What?*' She grabbed the key back from him and squinted at it.

'It was an easy mistake to make,' he told her. 'The number six is rather worn, so it looks like a five if you glance at it quickly.'

Josie swallowed hard. 'I—er—well, I suppose I ought to...'

'Apologise?' he finished for her smoothly, as her voice trailed away.

She definitely didn't want to apologise to this man, even though it looked as if she was the one who was in the wrong. She had to say something, though, and so she dug out a very half-hearted apology.

'This has all been my fault, after all. I'm sorry that I disturbed you.'

'If I hadn't been so tired, I might have enjoyed the disturbance rather more than I did,' he said in a voice that suddenly had silky undertones.

Josie picked up her bag and hastily backed towards the door. 'I'll—er—go to my own room, now.'

'Number sixteen,' he reminded her, his gold-brown eyes glinting.

'I know!' she snapped. Then she hurriedly stopped herself from saying anything more. She really wasn't in a position to be any more rude than she had been already.

'Perhaps you'd hang this on the door, on your way out.' He tossed something over to her. Josie caught it, and then looked at the neatly printed sign. "PLEASE DO NOT DISTURB" it said, in large, clear letters.

She gave a dark scowl. Oh, very funny! This man had a real sense of humour.

She glanced up at him, a cutting remark on the tip of her tongue. Then it went right out of her head as she saw that he was unzipping his jeans.

'What are you doing?' she yelped.

'Going back to bed,' he replied briefly. One well-shaped eyebrow gently rose. 'You are leaving—aren't you?'

She most certainly was! She moved out of room fifteen at top speed, and scooted along to her own room—number sixteen. As she opened the door, she found that she was holding her breath. What if someone else had made a similar mistake? She really didn't think she could go through all that again! To her relief, though, room sixteen was empty. She threw down her bag, and then found she was still holding the "PLEASE DO NOT DISTURB" sign. After a moment's thought, she hung it on her own door. Then she flopped down on to the bed, and let utter exhaustion sweep her into a deep sleep.

She slept right through the evening and the rest of the night. In fact, when she next opened her eyes daylight was filtering through the half-open shutters again, as another hot, humid day began in Calcutta.

Josie slowly hauled herself out of bed, still feeling heavy-eyed despite all the hours she had been asleep. She wouldn't have minded staying in bed for another couple of hours, but that just wasn't possible. She had another plane to catch this morning, one which would fly her to her final destination—Bhutan.

'*Where?*' she had said, when Derek had first suggested it.

'Bhutan,' he had repeated cheerfully.

'I don't even know where it is!'

'You go to India, then head north, and stop just before you get to Tibet,' he had replied. 'It's a small country tucked into the Himalayas. Very few tourists go there—mainly because the Bhutanese very sensibly let only a limited number in. You'll love it.'

And since Josie always enjoyed travelling and seeing new places, she had been more than happy to go along with his suggestion. Only now she was just a ninety-minute plane ride away from Bhutan, and she was definitely beginning to have some hefty qualms about this trip. She had travelled around Europe on her own, but this wasn't anything like Europe. This was Asia, and it felt very foreign, very exotic, and quite different from anything she had experienced before. She had certainly never planned to come on her own, and, now that she was here, she was beginning to discover that she didn't like being on this trip by herself. That was another new experience for her. Although she was

a sociable girl, she usually never minded her own
company. That was one more thing that seemed to be
changing, though.

The shower in the bathroom worked only in tepid
spurts, which didn't improve her mood. Grumbling
under her breath, she wriggled into a thin cotton
blouse and skirt, and slid her feet into a pair of light
sandals. She dragged a comb through her tousled
blonde curls, peered at her face in the mirror and decided that it could just about get by without any make-
up. She was lucky enough to have good, clear skin,
and eyelashes and eyebrows that were several shades
darker than her hair, so they didn't need to be em-
phasised with extra colour.

She was starving hungry by now. The last meal she
had eaten had been on the plane, and she had been
too travel-weary by then to eat more than half of it.

Probably because the hotel catered to large numbers
of tourists, it offered a full English breakfast on its
menu. Josie ordered everything: eggs, bacon, tom-
atoes, sausages and fried bread, with hot buttered
toast and coffee to follow. By the time she had demol-
ished everything that had been put in front of her,
she felt very much better. She ordered one more round
of toast and another cup of coffee, and was just
spreading marmalade on the toast when she saw a
horribly familiar figure entering the dining-room.

The piece of toast dropped from her suddenly
nerveless fingers, and left butter and marmalade stains
over the immaculate tablecloth. Josie rubbed at them
with a napkin, which only seemed to make them
worse, and at the same time furtively tried to watch
the man who had just come into the dining-room.

There were several empty tables, and, to her relief, he seemed to be making for one of them.

There was no reason why he should come anywhere near her table, of course. In fact, he probably wanted to make very sure that he avoided her. Then, out of the corner of her eye, she saw him glance in her direction. Hurriedly, she stared down at the table-cloth. She certainly didn't want him to catch her looking at him. He might get entirely the wrong idea!

She began to eat a piece of toast, determined to concentrate on her breakfast, even if she wasn't enjoying it nearly as much as she had been a couple of minutes ago. She was just swallowing the mouthful of toast when the man slid into the empty chair opposite her.

The piece of toast immediately stuck in her throat, and Josie began to choke. The man got up and obligingly thumped her on the back and, after a lot of coughing and spluttering, she began to get her breath back. Her eyes were still streaming, though, so she couldn't see him properly as he sat down in the chair again. She knew, however, that he had just ruined what was left of her breakfast.

'What are you doing here?' she croaked angrily at him, her voice still hoarse from all that coughing.

'I'm about to order breakfast,' he said reasonably.

'I don't mean that! I mean what are you doing *here*, at this table? There are plenty of other places you could sit.'

He shrugged. 'I'm on my own, and you seem to be on your own. I thought that, since we've already shared a bed, we might as well share a table.'

'Will you keep your voice down?' she hissed at him, at the same time going bright scarlet as several heads near by turned to stare at them with some interest. 'And we did *not* share a bed. Don't you dare go around telling people that we did!'

'Did you have the English breakfast?' he asked, as if she hadn't said anything at all. 'Was it any good? If it was, I think I'll have the same.'

'I don't want to talk about food!' Josie almost howled at him. Then she realised that it was her voice that was attracting attention this time, with more people turning to stare at their table. She felt her cheeks burn even brighter and wanted to sink through the floor with embarrassment.

'I'm going,' she muttered, pushing her plate of half-eaten toast away.

'Because of me?' he enquired.

'Yes, because of you!' She glared at him. 'And I hope you choke on *your* breakfast,' she told him rudely, before getting up and flouncing out of the dining-room.

For a couple of minutes, she stood in the reception area, still hot and flustered from that encounter. As she calmed down just a fraction, she realised that she had behaved very badly, but she didn't much care. There was something about that man that really grated on her already raw nerve-ends.

The bright colour that had flooded her face slowly began to fade, and she decided to go back to her room and get ready to leave. The sooner she was out of this hotel—and well away from that man—the happier she would be.

She was just going towards the stairs, when she heard someone calling her name.

'Miss Saunders?' said the slightly harassed-sounding voice again.

Josie turned, and found herself facing an attractive older woman, with a clipboard and several files tucked under her arm.

'Yes, I'm Josie Saunders,' she said.

'Oh, good,' said the woman, with some relief. 'I've already seen all the other members of your party. You're the last one on my list.' As Josie gave her a rather puzzled look, she explained, 'I'm the local representative of the travel agency that arranged your holiday to Bhutan. I'm afraid there's been a slight hitch. You won't be able to leave this morning.'

'What kind of hitch?' asked Josie.

'Some technical problem with the plane. Nothing serious, but it'll take a few hours to put right. Your flight's been re-scheduled for tomorrow morning. I do apologise, and of course we've made arrangements for you to stay here, at the hotel, for the extra night.'

Josie thought of the man in the dining-room. He might also be staying here for another night, and she definitely didn't want to bump into him again. 'Isn't there another hotel I could stay at?' she asked.

The woman looked surprised. 'Well—not really. Is something wrong?' she asked. 'Isn't your room comfortable?'

She gave a small sigh. 'My room's fine. It's just—oh, it doesn't matter,' she said with some resignation. 'I don't mind staying here.'

Relief showed on the woman's face. 'It really would be quite difficult to get you into another hotel. And it would be rather inconvenient, as well, as all the rest of the people on your tour are staying here. And I'm sorry about the delay of your flight, but Calcutta's really a very interesting city. Quite fascinating, in fact, as long as you can cope with the crowds and the noise.'

'And the smells?' said Josie, with a faint grin.

The woman smiled back. 'You get used to it, after a while.'

'I'm only going to be here for a day,' Josie said. 'Is there anything in particular that I should try and see?'

'Why not just walk around and get the flavour of the place?' the woman advised. 'Some people love it, a lot of people hate it, but at least it's not the kind of place that you can ever feel indifferent about.' Then she glanced at her watch. 'I must go,' she said, 'I've got another party to herd on to a plane to Kathmandu, and some lost luggage to chase after.'

She hurried off, and Josie lingered in the reception area for a few more minutes. What did she want to do with the rest of the day? She didn't know. One thing she was sure of, though. She didn't want to spend it in the hotel.

She was half hoping that she would see some of the other people who were booked on the same package holiday as she was. Perhaps they would let her tag along with them, if they were taking a look around Calcutta. She didn't see any faces she recognised, though, and after a while she gave a small sigh and left the hotel by herself.

The first thing to hit her was the heat. After the air-conditioning inside the hotel, it was almost like a physical blow. And after the heat, it was the noise that assaulted her. The amount of traffic was quite incredible. Engines revved up, roared and spluttered, fumes filled the air, and a cacophony of horns blew constantly. Josie felt as if she wanted to put her fingers in her ears.

She began to walk, nervous at being in this incredibly confusing city on her own, but at the same time fascinated. It certainly wasn't the place to come if you didn't like crowds! she decided. Every inch of space seemed to be filled. Buckets hung over coal fires, the smoke from the fires mingling with the traffic fumes and adding to the haze that hung over the city. Roadside stalls had been set up, serving everything from hot tea, curried beans and *chapatis* to polyester shirts, plastic toys and religious ornaments. Where there were broken standpipes, people were washing themselves and their clothes, the women deftly changing from wet saris to dry ones without losing any of their natural modesty. There was obviously enormous poverty and yet a great vitality. Josie had never been in a city remotely like it.

At the same time, though, she felt ill at ease. She supposed it was because she felt even more on her own in this great mass of people. If she had had someone with her, someone to talk to and share the experience with, it would all have been so very different.

She walked on for a few more minutes, then abruptly stopped and decided to go back to the hotel. This was no good. She usually had a lot of self-confidence, and she was definitely the independent type, but right now it all seemed to be deserting her. She supposed it was because this definitely wasn't the kind of holiday to come on by yourself. Perhaps the delayed flight had been a blessing. It would give her time to decide whether she actually wanted to carry on with her trip to Bhutan.

It was the first time she had actually considered abandoning the holiday. Now that she had finally reached that point, though, she didn't know why she had forced herself to come on it in the first place. It had been a mixture of defiance and perversity, she supposed. And an underlying, simmering anger at the man who should have been here with her.

Still preoccupied with her thoughts, Josie turned round, intending to trace her steps back to the hotel. Instead, she bumped straight into the man who had been standing only inches behind her.

'Sorry...' she began. Then she saw the gold-brown eyes, the gold-brown hair, and her face immediately grew dark. 'You again!' she said explosively. 'Are you following me?'

'Yes,' he said calmly.

That briefly threw her. She hadn't expected him to admit it quite so readily.

'Why?' she demanded.

'I saw you walking out of the hotel on your own. I wondered where you were going. And why you were all by yourself.'

'I don't see that either of those things are any of your business,' she said icily.

He shrugged. 'You're probably right. But it isn't always wise to walk around a strange city on your own.'

'I'm perfectly capable of looking after myself. I'm a grown woman. I don't need anyone to hold my hand.'

Those disconcerting eyes of his slid over her assessingly. 'You're maybe twenty-three, twenty-four,' he guessed accurately. 'Most people are grown up by that age, but that doesn't mean they're capable of coping with a city like Calcutta. And you haven't told me yet *why* you're on your own.'

'I believe I've already told you that it's none of your business!' she retorted. 'Now, if you'll excuse me, there are places I want to go.'

He didn't budge an inch, though. 'Such as?' he asked.

Josie had read every page in the guidebook about Calcutta before coming here, but right now, with those gold-brown eyes fixed on her, she couldn't remember the name of one single place of interest.

'I don't have to tell you,' she muttered at last, very well aware that it was a pretty lame reply.

He looked at her consideringly. 'My guess is that you aren't going anywhere at all,' he said at last. 'Calcutta turned out to be more overwhelming than you expected, so you were about to head back to the hotel.'

'Very clever,' she said, in a totally unimpressed voice. 'Do you do any other tricks, apart from mind-reading?'

He almost smiled. Almost, but not quite. Josie suddenly had the feeling that this man's smile was extremely rare.

'I'll walk back to the hotel with you,' he said in a relaxed tone.

'There's no need for that.'

'I know there isn't. But I'd like to walk with you, all the same.'

'Why?' she demanded suspiciously.

His eyes glinted. 'It'll give me a chance to get to know you better.'

'I don't see why you should *want* to get to know me.'

One of his eyebrows gently rose. 'I should think most men would like to know more about a blonde who suddenly turns up in their bed.'

'Don't bring that up again!' Josie said fiercely. 'I've explained exactly what happened. And you know perfectly well that I'd never have got into that bed if I'd known you were in it! Now, if you don't mind, I'm going back to the hotel—and on my own. I don't want to get involved with any strange men. For all I know, you could be a pervert or a rapist. You're probably not,' she added rather hastily, as she saw a dangerous light begin to glow in his gold-brown eyes, 'but I don't believe in taking chances.'

'Then why come to a place like Calcutta? It's not a particularly dangerous city, but it's an odd place for a girl like you to come for a holiday.'

'I'm not on holiday,' she said defiantly. 'I'm on my honeymoon!'

The moment she said it, she regretted it. She hadn't meant to tell anyone the truth.

He began to look at her with new interest. 'I don't see any sign of a husband,' he remarked.

'That's because he decided he wanted to spend *his* honeymoon with someone else,' Josie said, with a dark scowl. 'He dumped me two weeks before the wedding. I decided that I might have missed out on being a bride, but I wasn't going to miss out on the honeymoon, as well. So I came without him!'

She had no idea why she was telling this man all these highly personal details. Perhaps it was because he was a stranger. It didn't matter what she said to him. Once she had left Calcutta, she was never going to see him again. And she did need to talk to someone.

There was so much anger and resentment still churning around inside her, absolutely bursting to get out.

'You don't seem particularly upset that your wedding was cancelled at the last moment,' he observed.

Josie flushed. 'I *am* upset,' she insisted. She knew that she wasn't telling the exact truth, though. Every time she thought of Derek, she glowered hotly, and if he had been standing in front of her she might well have been tempted to throw a fairly emotional scene. She wasn't sobbing into her pillow at night, pulling her hair out or feeling totally grief-stricken and wiped out, though. She knew she should be—but she wasn't.

'She wasn't even very pretty,' she muttered at last.

'Who wasn't?'

'The girl he went off with. The girl he threw me over for!'

'This is beginning to sound more like dented pride than a tragic love-affair,' he commented.

Josie threw a black look at him. 'If you can't be sympathetic, then just go away!'

'If you'd wanted sympathy, you'd have stayed at home and cried buckets all over the shoulders of your family and friends. You didn't do that, though,' he pointed out. 'Instead, you packed your things and set off on holiday.'

'This isn't a holiday,' Josie reminded him fiercely. 'I've already told you that. Do you know what Derek said to me?' she went on, her brows drawing together into a deep glare. 'He said that he wanted our honeymoon to be a memorable experience. Well, it's certainly turned out to be that. And the main reason I'm going to remember it is because not too many girls go off on their honeymoon without a husband!'

She stopped there rather abruptly. Too late, she realised that she had said far too much. What on earth had made her blurt out all these things to a total stranger? And one that she had first met in such embarrassing circumstances!

He didn't seem in the least perturbed by her outburst, though. Instead, he was looking at her thoughtfully, as if assessing her afresh. Finally, he spoke. 'How do you feel about men, at the moment? Men in general, I mean?'

'They're all rats,' she said promptly. 'I don't ever want to get involved with another man—they're not worth all the trouble and pain and heartache. From now on, I'm going to concentrate on work, my friends, and seeing the world. I'm not interested in love, sex or marriage, and I'm definitely not interested in men in any shape or guise. Put the sexiest, most gorgeous man you can find right in front of me, and I won't bat an eyelid. I won't even bother to look at him.'

'Well, I don't rate myself in that category,' he said drily, 'but you're certainly showing a fairly healthy lack of interest in me.'

'Sorry if that doesn't do much for your ego,' she said, with a complete lack of genuine apology.

To her surprise, his mouth twitched in that small movement that was almost, but not quite, a smile.

'On the contrary,' he said. 'You could be just the girl that I'm looking for. My name is Daniel Hayden, by the way. And I'd like to offer you a job.'

CHAPTER TWO

THE noise and confusion of Calcutta's crowded streets reached a new crescendo at that point, and Josie shook her head.

'I didn't quite catch that,' she said. 'It sounded as if you said you were offering me a job. What did you really say?'

Daniel Hayden showed the first brief signs of impatience. 'I *did* offer you a job.'

'But . . .' she began. Then she stopped. 'I'm on my honeymoon,' she reminded him. 'Anyway, I don't need a job.'

'What kind of work do you usually do?'

'Secretarial work, mainly. Although not run-of-the-mill stuff. I've worked in television, advertising and local radio, for stockbrokers, bankers and wheeler-dealers—I'll try anything that sounds interesting.'

'You move around a lot.'

'I do temporary work. I'm registered with a good agency, and they send me wherever they think I'll fit in. Usually, I'm only at a place for two or three weeks, although sometimes I'll stay longer if they want someone to fill in for a member of staff on extended sick-leave, or something like that.'

'Are you good at your job?'

'I've never had any complaints,' she said. 'In fact, quite a few companies have wanted me to stay on with them permanently.'

'But you always turned down their offers?'

Josie gave a small grimace. 'I've got itchy feet. I like moving around all the time. More than anything, I like to travel. That's why temporary work suits me. I can work hard and save up like mad for a few months, and then take off for a couple of weeks—or until the money runs out.'

'You've travelled a lot?'

'Not as much as I'd like. But I've seen most of Europe and I've even managed to get to America a couple of times. This is my first time in Asia, though.'

'What do you think of it?'

'It's slightly overwhelming,' she admitted. 'It's probably not a good place to come on your own. At least, not on a first visit.'

'You're with a package tour, though, aren't you?'

'Yes, I am,' she agreed. Then she suddenly looked at him with fresh suspicion. 'How did you know that?'

'I asked a few questions at the hotel. I wanted to know what you were doing here. And where you were heading.'

'Why?' she demanded.

Daniel Hayden shrugged. 'Curiosity, in the beginning. Then, when I found you were on your way to Bhutan, it occurred to me that we might come to some sort of agreement.'

She looked at him sharply. 'You're going to Bhutan, as well?' When he nodded, she frowned. 'But you're not booked on the same package tour.'

'No,' he agreed, 'I'm making my way there independently.'

'You can't be,' she said promptly. 'Bhutan has very strict rules about tourists. You can only go there as part of an officially recognised holiday party.'

'I'm not a tourist. And I'm going to Bhutan at the special invitation of one of the princesses.'

Jose gave a disbelieving snort. 'Come on, do you really think I'm going to swallow that? How on earth would you know a Bhutanese princess?'

'Over the years, I've met quite a few interesting— and influential—people,' he said calmly. 'And I've an aunt staying in Calcutta at the moment with a friend of hers, a Maharaja. She's helped to arrange the visit for me, and cut through a lot of the red tape.'

His gold-brown gaze looked levelly into hers as he spoke, and Josie wrinkled her nose. Either he was telling the truth, or he could lie with such unnerving success that no one would ever be able to *tell* he was lying.

All the same—invited to Bhutan by a princess? His aunt friendly with a Maharaja? She wasn't sure she believed a word of it!

'I'm going to visit my aunt this evening,' he went on. 'Why don't you come along, and meet her? You'll be perfectly safe,' he added, his eyes gleaming. 'She's extremely respectable.'

'Unlike you, I suppose,' Josie muttered.

'I can be perfectly respectable, as well—when I put my mind to it. And I think you'd enjoy meeting my aunt. Like you, she loves to travel. In fact, my entire family does. I've got a couple of brothers, aunts, uncles, and a handful of cousins scattered all over the world. You hardly ever find any of my family at home. How about you?' he asked conversationally. 'Does your family like to travel?'

'I don't have a lot of family,' she said. 'Just my parents and a couple of elderly aunts. My parents have never been out of England. I don't know where I get my itchy feet from. My mother's convinced I'm a changeling, because I'm not in the least like either of them.'

'No, I don't think you're a changeling,' he said, his gaze resting on her assessingly. 'According to folklore, a changeling is a stupid, ugly child, left in place of a beautiful, clever one. I don't think that description fits you at all.'

Josie felt a hint of colour creeping into her face, which rather annoyed her. Surely she was old enough and mature enough to accept compliments without getting confused and flustered?

'You haven't told me yet why you're going to Bhutan,' she said rather hurriedly, deciding it was time to change the subject. 'If you're not a tourist, what's taking you to such an out-of-the-way country?'

'There's a strong possibility that I'll be making a film about it—a documentary.'

'For television?' she asked, immediately interested. 'Do you work for one of the TV companies?'

'No, I run a small film company of my own. We produce freelance films, mainly documentaries, and sell them to whoever's interested in buying them. At the moment, it's mainly the major TV companies, but as satellite TV catches on and expands, that should broaden the markets still further.'

'Why make a film about Bhutan?'

'Because it's a rather beautiful and fascinating place that most people know nothing about.'

'Wouldn't it be better if it stayed that way?' she said doubtfully. 'The Bhutanese don't want to be overrun by tourists.'

'It's very unlikely that my documentary will persuade hundreds of people to hop on to the nearest plane to Bhutan,' he said drily. 'Anyway, no definite decision about the film has been made yet. That's why I'm travelling there, to look around and see if it's a practical proposition. It's also why I'd like to take you with me. My personal assistant had to drop out at the last moment. She fell down a flight of steps and broke her leg.'

'Couldn't you find a replacement for her before you left England?'

'There wasn't time. Anyway, Margaret is very nearly irreplaceable. She's loyal, hard-working, dedicated—the perfect assistant.'

'She sounds like an absolute paragon,' Josie said with a small sniff. 'If she's that devoted to you, I'm surprised she didn't haul herself out here on a pair of crutches. She doesn't sound like the kind of girl who would let a little thing like a broken leg keep her away from her work.'

'As a matter of fact, she wanted to do precisely that,' Daniel said calmly. 'I had quite a job persuading her that it wasn't very practical to try and hop around Bhutan with one leg completely encased in plaster.'

Josie was fairly certain that she could picture the missing Margaret in her mind. A sweet, perhaps rather plain girl, who worshipped every inch of ground that Daniel Hayden walked on. Well, *she* wasn't that type of girl. And she had no intention of ever becoming one!

'Well, I'm sorry that your assistant couldn't come with you, but I really don't think I'd be a suitable replacement,' she said firmly. 'For a start, I don't know the first thing about making films.'

'You don't have to. I simply want someone to deal with the practical details, and to take notes as I travel around Bhutan.'

'I'm going there to relax and enjoy myself,' she reminded him. 'Not to work.'

'It wouldn't take up too much of your time. You'd still be able to fit in plenty of sightseeing. And I can take you to parts of Bhutan that you wouldn't see on a package tour,' he said persuasively. 'For example, the monasteries and temples have recently been closed to tourists, but I've managed to get special permission to go inside. You'd be able to see them properly, instead of just staring at them from the outside.'

For just a moment, Josie wavered. Then she firmly shook her head.

'I don't want to work for you,' she repeated.

All the time they had been talking, they had been walking slowly back to the hotel. They had reached it now, and went into the reception area.

Daniel Hayden stopped and turned to face her. 'Before you make a final decision, come and visit my aunt tonight,' he said. 'I'll meet you in the lobby, at seven, and take you there.'

'I *have* made a final decision,' Josie said, rather crossly. 'Meeting your aunt won't make me change my mind about anything.'

'Oh, I don't know,' he said, his gold-brown eyes briefly gleaming. 'She might be able to convince you that I'm not a rapist or a pervert. Seven o'clock,' he reminded her smoothly, and then he quickly walked off before she could tell him that she definitely didn't want to go anywhere with him.

Josie went up to her room in an increasingly bad temper. Really, that man was assuming just too much! She had only had a couple of brief—and fairly fraught!—meetings with him, and yet there he was, trying to get her to take a job that she didn't even want, and determined to make her meet his wretched aunt.

She headed straight for the shower, pulling off her clothes, which were clinging damply to her. Despite the air-conditioning inside the hotel, she didn't feel much cooler than she had in those hot, crowded streets outside.

The water trickled out a fraction faster than it had this morning, but it still took ages to finish showering and wash her hair. As she rubbed her blonde curls dry, she scowled at her reflection in the mirror.

She *didn't* want to go to Bhutan with Daniel Hayden, and she *didn't* want to meet his wretched aunt. But neither did she want to stay here on her own any longer.

So, what did she want? 'I want Derek,' she muttered, her voice suddenly cracking. Two large tears rolled down her face, followed by half a dozen more. 'He ought to be here,' she sniffled to herself. 'He shouldn't be planning his wedding to some mousy-haired girl he only met a couple of weeks ago. He should be here, married to me!'

She still hadn't got over the shock of it. She remembered exactly how he had looked, the day he had gently told her he was breaking off their engagement.

'But it's only two weeks to the wedding,' she had said with a mixture of total disbelief and panic.

'I know. And I'm really sorry. But I've just met this girl, and she's the one, Josie. I've always been so fond of you, we get along well together, we like the same things, and I thought those were the things you could build a good marriage on. But this is different. I took one look at Fern, and I knew she was the one I wanted to spend the rest of my life with.' He had lifted his shoulders in a slightly bewildered shrug. 'I don't understand it, but I know I'm doing the right thing. One day, the same thing will happen to you, and you'll know what I'm talking about—and perhaps forgive me, just a little.'

Josie remembered how angry she had been. She also remembered how she had gone to the building where Fern worked, and hidden behind a large plant in the foyer, determined to get a look at this girl who had taken Derek away from her. She had had no idea what she intended to do, once she had seen her. Confront her, perhaps? Demand that she give Derek back? But when she had finally set eyes on Fern she had been too staggered to do anything.

The girl had been downright plain! Mousy hair, and big brown eyes set in a thin, pale face. How could Derek have fallen so hard and so quickly for someone so very ordinary?

Josie hadn't understood any of it. She still didn't understand it.

She sat on the bed, slowly rubbing her damp curls. The half a dozen tears had dried up now, and no more had come to take their place. She hadn't cried properly since Derek's announcement. A couple of times she had tried to, because she had thought it would make her feel better, but the tears just wouldn't come.

Perhaps it was because she hadn't really loved Derek enough to waste useless tears over him, suggested a small voice inside her head.

'I did love him!' Josie said fiercely out loud. 'I *did*.'
Yet, somehow, there was a lack of conviction in her
voice. Perhaps it was because there had never been
any great passion between them. Theirs had been a
relaxed, comfortable relationship. She had always felt
at ease with Derek, and they had certainly shared a
love of travelling. She had first met him on a train
crossing Europe, when she had been on her way back
home from a summer in Italy and he had been back-
packing in the Alps. They had become friends, and
then more than friends. She had looked forward to
spending the rest of her life with him—but now he
wasn't there any more.

So, why didn't she feel totally devastated? She certainly ought to. Instead, she was angry and upset and
lonely, but she had the feeling that she was eventually
going to get over that. And perhaps even sooner than
she had expected.

'I did love him,' she muttered again. But there were
a lot of different kinds of love. There was the gentle
sort of love that you felt for a good, close friend—
like Derek—and the other kind; the kind that knocked
you right off your feet. For some inexplicable reason,
that was the way he felt about doe-eyed Fern. Josie
decided that she didn't ever want to feel that way
about anyone. It was too uncontrollable, too dangerous. Anyway, she had given up men! she reminded
herself. One bad experience was enough. She wasn't
risking anything like that happening again.

She slowly dressed and, without much pleasure,
thought about lunch, which would have to be eaten
alone. Then, after an afternoon by herself and another
lonely meal this evening, she would spend one last

night in this hotel before being whisked off to Bhutan in the morning.

Did she really want to go? Yes, she did, she realised. The soles of her feet were itching again. She wanted to see this small country tucked away in the folds of the Himalayas. Westerners called it Bhutan. The Bhutanese themselves called their country Druk Yul—the Land of the Thunder Dragon. Now that she had come this far, Josie didn't want to go home without seeing it.

Well, she could see it, she reminded herself. The package tour left in the morning. Except that she hated package tours. They were too regimented; they left too little time for any exploration she wanted to make on her own. And she particularly disliked this one because she was going to be the odd person out. The only one who was travelling alone. Some of the others might feel sorry for her and take her under their wing, but somehow that would just make it even worse.

Well, there was a solution to that, the little voice inside her head said persuasively. Travel with someone who's got permission to go wherever he likes. Someone who won't stick to a strict timetable, who can go right inside the fabulous monasteries. Someone who actually knows a Bhutanese princess.

'But I don't want to go with Daniel Hayden,' Josie said to herself irritably. 'Anyway, he's a stranger. I can't go waltzing off to the middle of nowhere with a stranger!'

When it came down to it, though, it seemed that she had a straight choice. Daniel Hayden, or the package tour.

Anyone with any sense would choose the package tour, she told herself more than once. No one in their right mind would go with someone like Daniel Hayden.

All the same, perhaps it wouldn't hurt to meet this aunt of his. Learn more about him, so that she could finally convince herself that the package tour was the wise choice—the only choice.

She kept changing her mind right through the afternoon. First, she would decide to go tonight. Then she would tell herself that she was going to stay right here, and that she wanted nothing more to do with either Daniel Hayden or his wretched aunt. All the same, when seven o'clock finally came round, she found herself heading towards the lobby, even though a part of her was still warning her that this definitely wasn't a good idea.

Daniel was already there, waiting for her. 'Good, you're on time,' he said briskly. 'I don't like unpunctuality. No one lasts long working for me unless they regularly turn up in the right place at the right time.'

'I haven't said I'm going to work for you,' Josie retorted with some annoyance. 'I haven't even said I'm coming with you this evening. For all you know, I might have come down to tell you that I intend to spend the evening at the hotel.'

His gaze slid over her. She was wearing the one good dress she had brought with her, a black, close-fitting and rather slinky little number. Her gold curls had dried to a bright halo, and her dark blue eyes were highlighted with skilful use of mascara and subtle eyeshadow.

'If you're planning on eating in the hotel diningroom, that outfit might distract rather a lot of men from their food,' he commented.

'*You* don't look very distracted,' she pointed out, and then regretted that remark. It sounded as if she were fishing for compliments, and she most certainly wasn't.

Daniel merely shook his head. 'You're right, I'm not in the least distracted. Nor am I interested in what you look like, although I can appreciate the fact that most men would give you a second and a third look.'

'Then what does interest you about me?' she demanded. 'I'd have been quite happy if I'd never seen you again, after that pretty embarrassing incident in the hotel bedroom. You keep popping up all over the place, though. Every time I turn round, you seem to be a couple of feet behind me.'

'Pure coincidence,' he said calmly. 'But you're right, there was something about you that interested me. It was the fact that you'd come all this way by yourself. Anyone who tackles that kind of trip has to be fairly independent, and have a certain amount of self-confidence and self-reliance. Those are the qualities I look for in the people I employ. That's why I decided that there was a good chance you'd make an ideal temporary assistant, for my trip to Bhutan.'

Josie felt just a little outraged. This man was so cool! He didn't seem to see the human qualities in people. He only looked for efficiency and productiveness; for someone who would make the perfect employee.

On the other hand, she argued with herself, wasn't this exactly the kind of man she could get along with? Someone who didn't see her as an individual person, but as a working partner? She was through with personal relationships with men. None of them could be trusted, she was convinced of it. She could hardly avoid them for the rest of her life, though, so why not work for a man who seemed completely uninterested in her, as a person? It could well turn out to be the ideal sort of partnership.

She wasn't stupid or naïve, though. She wasn't going to go waltzing off to the back of beyond with someone she knew virtually nothing about. Before she reached any final decision she would have a long talk with this aunt of his, and find out just what type of person she would be working for.

'If we stand around much longer, we're going to be late,' she said briskly. 'And if your aunt's as keen on punctuality as you are, she isn't going to appreciate that.'

'My aunt's a lot more relaxed than I am about most things,' he said, with a touch of amusement. 'But I'm ready to leave, if you are. I've got a taxi waiting outside.'

It had been raining heavily during most of the afternoon, and, although it had stopped now, the humid dampness added a new dimension to the smells that drifted through the streets. Josie was glad that she had generously squirted perfume over herself before dressing.

She scrambled into the taxi, and Daniel got in beside her. Unlike her, he hadn't made any attempt to dress up for this meeting with his aunt. He was still wearing denims—although a less scruffy pair than he had had on this morning—and his only concession to any kind of formal dress was the white shirt he wore with it. Even that was open at the neck, showing rather more supple, tanned skin that Josie wished to see.

The taxi tore through the packed streets of Calcutta at a quite suicidal speed. She gritted her teeth, and told herself that she wasn't absolutely terrified at the way the driver was missing people, animals, cars and trucks by just fractions of an inch.

'Driving through Calcutta is always an interesting experience, isn't it?' Daniel said, his eyes glinting.

'That rather depends on what you consider to be interesting,' Josie got out through tense lips.

'Don't worry. It isn't much further.'

'I'm not worried,' she denied at once. Then she briefly closed her eyes as the driver swerved round a herd of animals wandering across the road. 'It's just that I'd like to get there without a goat stuck on the bonnet, like some gory mascot!'

To her relief, the taxi seemed to be rattling into a part of the city which was much quieter and emptier. The houses were whitewashed, large and well-to-do, and no one lived on the pavements, sold things from the street corners or ran up to the car, begging.

A few minutes later, the driver headed the car through wide entrance gates and pulled up outside a house that was almost grand enough to be considered a small mansion. Daniel got out and paid the driver. Josie climbed out more slowly, staring up at the house with some surprise.

'This is where your aunt is staying?' When he nodded, she went on, 'Why aren't you staying here, with her? It would certainly be an improvement on the hotel!'

'The house doesn't belong to my aunt. She's here as a guest of the Maharaja, who owns it.'

Josie's eyebrows rose expressively. 'Your aunt seems to have some very influential friends!'

'She certainly knows some interesting people,' Daniel agreed. 'Are you coming inside? I think it's going to rain again.'

Since it didn't just rain in India during the monsoon season, but came down in great sheets that soaked everything in seconds, Josie scurried after him as he headed towards the front entrance.

The door opened even before they reached it, and a man in a white jacket, white trousers and white gloves greeted them formally.

'Mr Hayden?' he said very politely. 'Please come inside, with your guest.'

'Who's he?' whispered Josie, as she followed Daniel inside. 'The Maharaja?'

Daniel's eyes registered amusement. 'No,' he said, in an equally low voice. 'He's the Indian equivalent of the butler. As a matter of fact, the Maharaja isn't even here. When I phoned my aunt earlier, to let her know we'd be coming, she told me he was away on business.'

'Oh,' she said with some disappointment. She had been looking forward to meeting a real Maharaja.

They were led into a room that was furnished in a very modern style. Josie was disappointed all over again. She had hoped for something a lot more exotic.

'Where's your aunt?' she asked.

'Probably still getting ready,' replied Daniel. 'She loves dressing up.'

A few moments later, the door opened and a tall woman swept in, wearing a gorgeous, gold-trimmed sari. She certainly wasn't Indian, though. Her skin and hair were fair, and her eyes, as she looked straight at them, were a familiar gold-brown. Did tiger eyes run in the Hayden family? Josie wondered irrelevantly. Then Daniel gently pushed her forward, to meet his aunt.

'Daniel!' said his aunt, her gaze sweeping over him. 'You're wearing jeans. Now that I think of it, I don't believe I've ever seen you in a proper suit.'

'Sorry,' he said cheerfully. 'Jeans were all I brought with me on this trip. They're very clean and quite respectable, though.'

His aunt's gaze remained disapproving, but her mouth relaxed into a smile as she turned to Josie. 'And who have you brought with you?' she asked her nephew.

'This is...' began Daniel. Then he stopped and looked at Josie a little blankly. 'I don't know your name.'

She couldn't stop a grin spreading across her face. 'I thought you didn't. I've never told you, and you've never asked.' Then she turned back to Daniel's aunt. 'I'm Josie Saunders,' she introduced herself.

'And I'm Katherine Hayden,' replied his aunt. 'I'm delighted to meet you, and I apologise for the appalling manners of my nephew.'

To Josie's astonishment, Daniel didn't take any offence. Instead, he looked at his aunt with unexpected affection. 'If you're going to lecture me all evening, I think I need a drink. Or perhaps even two.'

'Daniel,' said his aunt warningly.

'Don't worry,' he replied calmly. 'I can easily stop at two now.'

Josie's brows drew together fractionally. What were they talking about? Had there been a time when he *couldn't* stop at two drinks? And if not, why?

She almost asked the questions out loud, only just stopping herself in time. It was none of her business, she reminded herself sternly. And Daniel Hayden didn't strike her as the kind of man who would appreciate a virtual stranger probing into any problems he might have once had.

'Are you hungry?' asked his aunt. 'Dinner's ready. We can eat straight away.'

She opened mahogany doors which led into a dining-room, where the table was already laid with a selection of hot dishes and salads. Josie had a healthy appetite, and she ate everything that was served on to her plate.

'Tell me something about yourself,' said Daniel's aunt after a while, looking at Josie. 'Daniel's told me absolutely nothing about you.'

'That's because I don't know anything,' Daniel interrupted. 'Except that she's on a honeymoon trip to Bhutan.'

Josie immediately glared at him. She hadn't wanted anyone to know about that, not even his aunt. She certainly wished she hadn't blurted it out to *him*.

His aunt looked at her with new interest. 'A honeymoon trip? But where's your husband? Why didn't you bring him with you tonight?'

'Because I haven't *got* a husband,' Josie muttered. 'We split up just before the wedding. In fact, next week he's marrying someone else. I came on the honeymoon without him.'

She flinched a little as she waited for the inevitable sympathy. Instead, though, Daniel's aunt gave a small shrug that was rather unnervingly reminiscent of the shrug she had seen Daniel give several times.

'That sounds like a very sensible thing to do. Why miss out on a perfectly good honeymoon just because you haven't got a husband? Daniel, you've finally found a girl who's got a lot of common sense.'

'I know,' he agreed. 'That's why I want her to come and work for me. First of all, though, she wants to know more about me. I'm relying on you to give me a good character reference.' Then his gold-brown eyes altered a little as he looked directly at his aunt. 'She'll be *working* for me,' he repeated, with a slight emphasis on the word 'working'. 'If she agrees to it, it'll be a temporary arrangement. I just want you to convince her that she'll be quite safe, wandering off into the wilds of Bhutan with me.'

His aunt looked at Daniel through narrowed eyes for a few moments. Then she nodded. 'I understand.'

Josie wished that *she* understood. There were private messages being sent between the two of them, and she had no idea what they were. That definitely unsettled her. What was going on here?

His aunt Katherine was already speaking again, though. 'Why don't you take yourself off for a few minutes, Daniel?' she suggested. 'I think it would be better if I talked to Josie on her own.'

Josie had the impression that Daniel wasn't very keen on that idea. It was almost as if he was afraid of what his aunt might tell her. In the end, though, he slowly got up and walked towards the door. 'All you need to give her is a character reference,' he repeated again in a warning tone. Then, with obvious reluctance, he left the room.

His aunt smiled at Josie in a relaxed manner. 'All right, what do you want to know about Daniel? Just remember that I won't answer any questions that are too personal.'

Josie grimaced. 'I'm not sure *what* I want to ask. I'm not even sure I want to work for him. After all, I'm meant to be on holiday.'

'Oh, you'll enjoy the trip a lot more if you go with Daniel,' said his aunt firmly. 'He'll take you to places that you'd never get to see on an ordinary package tour.'

'I might be a lot safer on a package tour,' Josie pointed out.

'That depends on what you mean by safe,' replied his aunt, in an unperturbed tone. 'I'm not saying that Daniel doesn't occasionally get into sticky situations. When you travel as much as he does, that's bound to happen. But you certainly don't have to worry about your personal safety. He won't jump on you the moment that you leave civilisation behind.'

Josie felt herself growing rather hot. 'I didn't think that he would,' she denied. Then she gave a wry grimace. 'Well, yes, I did,' she admitted. 'After all, I really don't know him. I've no idea *what* he might do.'

'He'll probably work you very hard, but that's all.' His aunt hesitated for a moment, then added, 'I probably shouldn't tell you this—but I will, since it might make you feel better about the situation. Daniel isn't interested in women, at the moment.'

Josie's eyes flew wide open. 'Not interested?' she said in astonishment. 'You mean he's——?' She broke off very hurriedly and went bright scarlet. She definitely had no right to ask that question!

His aunt was looking very amused now. In fact, her mouth was rising at the corners into the kind of smile that Daniel might have given, if he were a man who ever smiled.

'Daniel most certainly *likes* women,' she said. 'What I said was, he isn't interested in them right now. He doesn't want to get involved in any kind of relationship.'

'Well, I can understand that,' Josie said promptly. 'I feel exactly the same way about men. I don't mind talking to them, or working with them, but that's it. I don't want any kind of relationship that isn't very strictly platonic.'

'In that case,' said his aunt gravely, 'it rather sounds as if the two of you are made for each other. I'll bring Daniel back and tell him that he's found the perfect assistant for himself.'

'I still haven't definitely decided to take the job,' Josie said rather defiantly.

'Of course you have,' replied his aunt, in a no-nonsense voice. 'If you didn't intend to take it, you wouldn't have come here tonight. You just needed to reassure yourself that Daniel wasn't *too* disreputable or untrustworthy.'

'I'm still not absolutely certain that he isn't either of those things,' Josie muttered.

'What things?' enquired Daniel, making her jump. She hadn't heard him come silently back into the room.

'It's all right,' said his aunt Katherine. 'Josie's going to work for you, although she's still rather reluctant to admit it.'

'Good,' he said briskly. 'Let's just hope that the plane leaves in the morning without any more delays. I can't afford to waste too much time on this project.'

Josie felt as if everything was moving rather too fast. These Haydens seemed to be bulldozing her into this, and not giving her any chance to back out.

'If I do take this job, I've a condition to make,' she said, staring straight at Daniel.

His gold-brown eyes looked calmly back at her. 'What condition?'

'If it doesn't work out—if we don't get on, or I can't do the job well enough to satisfy you—you don't just dump me in the middle of Bhutan, and leave me there.'

'That seems fair enough,' he agreed, after a moment's hesitation. 'All right, no matter what happens, I promise to deliver you safely back here, to Calcutta, where you can get a flight home to England. Does that satisfy you?'

Josie wasn't sure that it did, but she didn't know quite what else she could demand from him. 'I suppose so,' she muttered at last.

'Then we leave in the morning, for Bhutan,' he said with some satisfaction.

Josie couldn't quite get rid of the feeling that she had made a wrong decision somewhere along the line. That, even now, it would be a good idea to change her mind and stick to the package tour. Instead, though, she found herself nodding rather feebly.

'We'll leave in the morning,' she echoed. And she tried hard to ignore the hefty twitch that her nerve-ends gave as she said those words.

CHAPTER THREE

Josie arrived at the airport the next morning, with Daniel Hayden, and tried hard to ignore the curious looks that she was getting from the people booked on the package tour to Bhutan. They had known she was booked on that same tour. Now, though, she had suddenly deserted it, and was travelling to Bhutan with a man she had only just met. She could guess what they were saying in low voices, behind her back!

She supposed it didn't help that Daniel was a very eye-catching man. Tall, fairly powerfully built, with those gold-brown colourings, he was definitely the type people would notice—particularly women.

'All of these people know that we only met in Calcutta,' she muttered under her breath. 'They think we're about to embark on some exotic affair!'

'Whatever they think, it doesn't bother me,' replied Daniel, in a slightly bored voice. Then his eyes narrowed slightly. 'Does it bother you?'

'Certainly not,' she said sturdily, and she stared a little defiantly at the people around them, forcing them to look away with just a touch of embarrassment.

As they walked out to the plane, which was waiting on the runway, Josie stopped worrying about the softly spoken comments and the gossip. Instead, she stared at the plane, which had the saffron and orange Bhutanese thunder dragon painted on its tail.

'It doesn't look very big,' she said uneasily.

'What were you expecting?' said Daniel, with that glitter in his eyes that was the nearest he came to any open sign of amusement. 'A jumbo jet? Visitors to Bhutan are fairly thin on the ground. A plane this size is quite big enough to cope with them.'

Josie would still have felt much happier in something a lot larger. She clambered aboard, though, beginning to feel rather fatalistic about this entire journey. Perhaps some of the Eastern attitude to life was beginning to rub off on her!

The plane lumbered into the air and began to fly northwards, with the flat plains of Bengal spread out below them. Because it was the time of the monsoon, there were great sheets of water covering much of the ground, with roofs and palm trees sticking out above the flood water.

'What exactly do you want me to do, when we reach Bhutan?' asked Josie, finally tearing her gaze away from the window and turning to Daniel.

He had his eyes closed, although he wasn't asleep. When she spoke to him, he opened them, and she was struck all over again by their colour. She had never seen a man with eyes quite like his before.

'What do I want you to do?' he echoed. 'Just generally organise things, and leave me free to get on with my job.'

'And what exactly is your job? I mean, what will *you* be doing when we get there?'

'I'll be looking for good locations, for filming, I'll be talking to people and getting a general idea of what they think and feel about their country, and I'll be planning a general outline of the documentary—assuming that everything works out, and it actually gets off the ground. One thing I would like from you—if you can manage it,' he added, 'is some female input.'

'Some *what*?' she said a little blankly.

He gave a slightly impatient sigh. 'Female input. Isn't that self-explanatory?' Seeing that it wasn't, he went on, 'Women, as well as men, watch documentaries. I'll be looking at the country from a strictly male point of view. It's a well-known fact that men and women see things very differently, so I want to know what *you* see when you look at Bhutan.'

Josie looked at him curiously. 'Do you really believe men and women look at things in such very different ways?'

'I believe we're two completely different races,' he said flatly. 'And with frighteningly little in common.' Then, as if he had said far more than he had meant to, he gave a brief shake of his head. 'But that's irrelevant. Are you willing to try and give me that kind of input?'

'I suppose so,' she said, with a grimace. 'Although I doubt if you'll end up using any of it.'

Daniel looked surprised. 'Why do you say that?'

'Because you strike me as the type of man who likes to put his own individual stamp on his work. Whether you intend it or not, I'll bet that documentary ends up giving *your* view of Bhutan, and no one else's.'

'I work as part of a team,' he said briefly.

'But if you own the company, then you must be the head of that team,' Josie pointed out.

'Do you think I'm dictatorial? That I never listen to anyone else's ideas or points of view?' He was frowning rather darkly now.

Josie decided that it might be a good idea to stop this conversation right here. There was no point in ruffling his temper before they even reached Bhutan!

'I'm sure you're the perfect employer,' she said soothingly. Then she turned towards the window. 'Look,' she said, determined to change the subject, 'those must be the foothills of the Himalayas.'

The plane was climbing upwards now, the engines sounding just a little too laboured for Josie's liking. To try and stop herself from feeling nervous, she gazed out at the view below.

There was quite a lot of heavy cloud, but through the occasional breaks in it she could catch tantalising glimpses of dense forest, valleys, and rivers. The mountains were getting higher, and sometimes seemed perilously close. Josie chewed her lip a little nervously, and then turned back to Daniel.

'Shouldn't the plane be trying to gain more height? It doesn't look as if it's going to make it over that next range of mountains!'

'It's about as high as it can go. And don't look so worried. I believe the plane usually makes it to Bhutan in one piece.'

'Usually?' Josie gulped. 'I'd feel a lot happier if you could be a bit more positive than that!'

She gazed out at the mountains, which were looming much nearer now. She was *sure* they weren't going to make it over the top. The plane seemed to be skimming the very tips of the trees, and Josie closed her eyes.

A few seconds later, Daniel lightly touched her arm. 'You can open your eyes again now. We'll be coming in to land very soon.'

Cautiously, she glanced out of the window. Miraculously, they had cleared the mountains and were sweeping down towards a wide valley. Josie saw the gilded roofs of a temple, with flags fluttering from its ramparts, and then white farmhouses and bright green paddy fields. What she *couldn't* see was an airstrip.

'Where are we going to land?' she asked nervously.

'Down there,' said Daniel, pointing.

She peered out, but couldn't see anything except boggy fields of rice. Then, at the very last moment, a narrow strip of dry land appeared in front of them, and the plane touched down on it safely.

A few minutes later, Josie got off the plane and set foot in Bhutan for the first time—the Land of the Thunder Dragon.

The first thing that struck her was the air. It was clear and pure. Very different from the humid heat, the smells and the fumes of Calcutta! And everywhere seemed so green and fresh, against the background of densely forested mountains.

There were a couple of minibuses, waiting for the passengers from the plane.

'Where are we going?' asked Josie, as she climbed aboard one of them and sat down beside Daniel.

'To Thimphu, the capital,' he told her.

Josie gave a rather relieved sigh. She immediately had visions of hot baths, soft beds, and shops she could browse around in any spare time Daniel Hayden might allow her.

'Don't get too excited,' Daniel told her. 'Thimphu might be the capital, but it's still only got a population of around fifteen thousand. Of course, by Bhutanese standards, that's quite crowded.'

'Just as long as it's got a hotel with a comfortable room,' Josie said longingly.

'We were only on that plane for an hour and a half,' Daniel pointed out, with a small frown. 'If travelling for that short amount of time makes you tired, you aren't going to be much use to me over the next few days. I'll be covering a lot of distance, and there won't be much time for rest.'

'Travelling doesn't make me tired. It's being nervous that wears me out. And when that plane flew over the mountains I was *very* nervous,' she said, with some feeling.

The minibus rattled on through sparsely populated countryside, and occasionally, through the open windows, Josie could catch the musical sound of bells on prayer wheels. Although it wasn't late in the day, her eyes were beginning to feel distinctly heavy. She forced them open again, however, as they entered the long, narrow valley where Thimphu was situated. She didn't want to miss a moment of her arrival in Bhutan's tiny capital.

It was more like a town than a city. On either side of the valley were high hills covered with trees, with whitewashed houses dotted in among the greenery. But Thimphu itself was dominated by a great building with white-buttressed walls, towers, and gilded roof-tops, which overshadowed the small houses clustered around it.

'What's that?' asked Josie, fascinated.

'The Tashicho Dzong,' replied Daniel. 'It's part fortress and part monastery. It's the administrative centre of Bhutan, and also the headquarters of the monks.'

'Will we get a chance to have a closer look at it later?'

'We should be able to go right inside.'

'By special permission of this Bhutanese princess you're so friendly with?' asked Josie, with some scepticism.

'That's right,' he said in an unperturbed tone.

She gave a small snort. She wasn't at all sure she believed all these tales about the princess. In fact, there were a lot of things she wasn't sure about where Daniel Hayden was concerned!

A few minutes later, they reached their hotel. To her relief, they were the only two who got off the minibus. The package tour party were being taken on to another hotel.

Their bags were unloaded, and they carried them inside. Before Daniel went to register he turned and looked at her.

'I booked a room for myself, in advance. I'll have to try and get another room for you.' One gold-brown eyebrow gently rose. 'I assume you don't want to share?'

'No, I certainly don't!' Josie retorted at once.

'I didn't think that you would,' he said drily. 'Although that's something we'll have to talk about later.'

As he went to register, Josie looked after him warily. What did he mean, they would have to talk about it later? As far as she could see, there was nothing to discuss.

He came back with two keys in his hand. 'We're in luck. They had a spare room. We're on the first floor. Your room's at the front of the hotel, and mine's at the back.'

Josie was relieved to hear that. It sounded as if their rooms were some distance apart, which definitely suited her.

In fact, her room looked out over the main street, with its tea houses and shops. She quickly unpacked, feeling much less tired now that they were actually here, in Thimphu. She was just shovelling the last of her clothes into a drawer when there was a light tap on the door. Hoping that it would be one of the hotel boys bringing her a much needed cup of tea, she called for him to come in.

It wasn't one of the hotel boys. It was Daniel. He came into her room, closed the door behind him, and then looked around.

'Nice room,' he commented. 'But don't get too comfortable. We won't be staying in Thimphu for long. I'm on a fairly tight schedule.'

'Where are we going next?' she asked.

'Eastwards, I hope, to Tongsa and Bumthang. But that rather depends on the princess.'

The princess again—Josie gave a slightly irritable sigh. This man was a definite name-dropper!

'I suppose we're going to get a personal invitation to the palace, so she can explain the itinerary that she's personally worked out for you?' she said, with more than a touch of sarcasm.

'That's more than likely,' Daniel replied calmly.

Josie made a rather rude noise. She would believe in this princess when she finally came face to face with her.

'I'm starving,' she announced, changing the subject. 'Can we get something to eat here, at the hotel?'

'They've got a good restaurant. And I'd get as many decent meals in as you can while we're here. Once we leave Thimphu, we'll probably end up eating a great deal of rice. They eat huge amounts of it in Bhutan.'

'I don't mind,' Josie shrugged, 'I like rice.'

'You might be very tired of it by the time this trip is over,' he said drily. 'But I didn't come here to talk about food. There's something else I want to get sorted out before we go any further.'

His tone of voice seemed to change, making Josie look at him with suddenly narrowed eyes. Although she couldn't have explained why, she had the feeling that this conversation was about to get rather difficult.

'I thought that everything had been sorted out quite satisfactorily,' she said, her gaze becoming slightly wary.

'Not quite.' It was quite impossible to read what lay behind those gold-brown eyes. Even his voice gave nothing away. 'At the moment, we've managed to find a couple of rooms in a comfortable hotel, but once we get out into the countryside we're not likely to be this lucky.'

Josie shrugged. 'That's all right, I don't mind roughing it. I don't even mind sleeping out for the odd night, if the weather's reasonable. I've been camping several times before, and I've always managed perfectly well.'

'We should be able to find a room most nights,' said Daniel. 'But that's the point I'm trying to make. It might be just one room.'

At that, her dark blue eyes sharpened. 'You're telling me that we'll have to share it?'

'It's something that happens quite often, when you're working on location,' he said casually. 'I've often had to share sleeping accommodation with my staff in the past, and it's never caused any great problems on either side.'

He seemed to take such a relaxed attitude towards the prospect of their sharing a room that Josie didn't want to make a big thing of it, and make herself sound childishly immature in the process. On the other hand, she definitely didn't want to sleep in the same room as Daniel Hayden!

'Since it's something that might not even happen, why don't we just forget about it for now?' she suggested a little edgily, at last. 'We'll work something out if it actually turns out to be necessary.'

'That's OK by me,' Daniel agreed, to her relief. 'But I thought I ought to mention it, before we leave Thimphu. I don't want to have to deal with an outraged scene with you in a few days' time, if we end up in some remote village with only very limited accommodation.'

'I don't make outraged scenes,' Josie informed him, with icy dignity.

'I'm pleased to hear it,' he replied, in an equally cool tone. 'In that case, perhaps there's one more thing we ought to get out of the way, before we leave Thimphu.'

She wasn't at all sure that she wanted this conversation to go on for one minute longer. She could hardly order him out of her room, though, so instead she looked at him as levelly as she could.

'Well, what is it?' she said shortly.

'We're going to be spending rather a lot of time with each other over the next few days.'

'I know that. It isn't going to be a problem, is it?'

'It won't be, if we get a few ground rules sorted out right now. That way, it leaves no possible room for misunderstanding.'

'Misunderstanding about what?' she asked warily.

'Our relationship.'

Her dark blue eyes took on a warning glow. 'We don't have a relationship!'

'Precisely.' His own voice remained very cool. 'But that doesn't necessarily stop certain problems arising. That's why it would be much better to know right now if you're interested in sex.'

'What?' yelped Josie.

He remained totally unruffled. 'Don't look at me as if I'd just made an obscene suggestion. I'm merely being practical. Some women enjoy sex, and others don't. I just wondered which category you fell into.'

'I don't see that's any of your business!' she howled at him. 'And even if I do enjoy sex, that certainly doesn't mean I—I...'

'Want to jump into bed with me?' he finished for her, as she spluttered to a halt. He was almost smiling now. Almost, but not quite. 'I didn't really think that you would, but I wanted to make sure. You'd be surprised how many women have tried to crawl into my sleeping-bag, on trips of this kind.'

'Oh, I'm sure I'd be utterly amazed,' she retorted hotly. 'Why don't you tell me just *how* many there have been? You must have kept count. Or perhaps you're so incredibly popular that you just can't keep track of the numbers. Your women probably have to make an appointment to see you!'

His gold-brown eyes darkened a fraction. 'There aren't any women in my life right now,' he said, his voice abruptly sounding very brittle.

Josie suddenly remembered his aunt telling her that Daniel Hayden wasn't interested in women. 'Does that mean you're the kind of man who can't cope with relationships?' she said rather scornfully. 'You're only interested in casual sex?'

It struck her that this was a very odd conversation to be having with her employer. No one else she had worked for had spoken to her like this, or forced her into giving such personal replies. On the other hand, Daniel Hayden wasn't quite like anyone she had ever met before!

An angry gleam began to light up his eyes. 'I shouldn't have brought this subject up,' he muttered.

'No, you shouldn't. But, since you have, we might as well get this thing settled right now. You might want and enjoy casual sex, but I don't! Even if we have to share a room every night we're in Bhutan, I won't be crawling into your sleeping-bag. Am I getting through to you?' she demanded, her face still flushed with heat and anger.

He seemed to have regained control of his own temper without too much difficulty. He was a very cool man, she decided. No deep emotions, no real capacity to feel or respond or even smile.

'This whole thing has got blown up out of all proportion,' he said at last, after a brief pause. 'I simply wanted to know if you were the kind of girl who was interested in casual sex. You're obviously not, and I accept that.'

'And if I had been interested?' Josie couldn't stop herself asking.

He gave an offhand shrug. 'Then we might have found a few ways of livening up the long and boring nights. As it is, we'll stick to our own beds, and keep this a strictly working partnership.'

Josie gazed at him edgily. Was this man in the least trustworthy? Could she believe a single thing he said?

As if reading her mind, he looked at her levelly. 'Don't worry, you're perfectly safe,' he told her. 'I'm not interested in you, as a person. I'm not even interested in sex unless it's a simple two-way exchange of pleasure.'

His words should have been totally insulting. Instead, Josie discovered that there was something in the flat tone of his voice which struck an echoing note among her own exposed nerve-ends. It was the way *she* sometimes spoke, when she was trying to hide something too personal, too raw, to be discussed with any other person.

She shot a quick look at him. What was going on below that cool surface? she wondered. What secrets was he hiding?

None of your business, a brisk voice inside her head warned her. Don't even try to find out. Just get on with your job, or clear out altogether if you find this man too much to handle.

But Josie wasn't in the mood to admit that she had met a man she couldn't handle. Look on this job as a challenge, she instructed herself. A way of proving to yourself that you haven't lost all your self-confidence just because that rat of a fiancé dumped you for someone else!

'At least we've got a couple of things clear,' she said at last, in a voice that she somehow managed to keep as cool and detached as his own. 'I'm not interested in you, and you're not interested in me. That seems like a good basis for a working relationship, so let's get on with the job that we've come here to do.'

For just an instant, he looked surprised. 'No hysterics?' he said, his eyebrows lightly rising. 'No walking out, declaring that you can't work with a man like me?'

'I'm not the hysterical type. And as long as you remember I don't go for casual sex I don't see any reason to walk out.'

'I'm not likely to forget it,' said Daniel Hayden, his mouth twitching slightly.

Josie suddenly had the feeling that he was trying hard not to smile. That was ridiculous, of course, because she was quite sure that he *never* smiled. Anyway, she didn't see anything particularly funny about this situation.

'What are we going to do now?' she asked, feeling just a little on edge again.

'You can do whatever you like,' he told her. 'Personally, I'm going down to see if I can get something to eat. Do you want to come along?'

That was just like a man, Josie thought rather crossly. This distinctly odd conversation hadn't upset or bothered him one little bit. It hadn't even affected his appetite.

'I'm not hungry,' she muttered. 'I think I'll go out for a while, and take a look around Thimphu.'

'I'd prefer it if you stayed at the hotel. The princess could get in touch at any time. When she does send for us, it would be polite to go and see her straight away. I don't want to have to spend an hour wandering round Thimphu, looking for you.'

Josie shot him a sceptical look. 'I'm beginning to wonder if this princess actually exists! You keep talking about her, but there's been precious little sign of her so far.'

'You'll meet her soon enough,' he replied in a calm voice. 'In the meantime, you might as well come down to the dining-room with me and have something to eat.'

'It looks as if I don't have much choice,' she said, very ungraciously. 'After all, you do employ me. I suppose that gives you the right to tell me where I can or can't go, during working hours.'

'And since, on an assignment like this, we'll be working most hours of the day—and night—that means you're going to spend quite a lot of time doing exactly what I tell you,' he said, with another unexpected glimmer of amusement.

Josie didn't answer him. If she had, she would have said something very rude! Instead, she followed him down to the dining-room, scowling at his back.

The menu was more varied than she had expected, and the food good. Remembering Daniel's advice, she avoided any dishes including rice, and instead chose chicken served with lightly fried vegetables. She was determined not to let Daniel's presence ruin her appetite, and kept her gaze fixed firmly on her plate. If she didn't look at him, she could pretend he wasn't there. That helped her to get through the meal.

For his own part, Daniel didn't say a single word while they were eating. In the end, she glanced up at him and found that he wasn't paying the slightest attention to her. In fact, she had the rather unsettling feeling that he had forgotten she was even there.

Towards the end of the meal, one of the hotel staff came over and discreetly murmured something in

Daniel's ear. His gold-brown eyes immediately became alert again, and he nodded briefly to Josie.

'This is it,' he told her. 'The summons from the princess. She's sent a car for us.'

Josie blinked. 'A car?'

'How did you think we were going to get there?' he said, with a touch of exasperation. 'By yak?'

He got up and began to leave the dining-room, leaving Josie to scuttle along behind him.

'Where does she live?' she asked a little breathlessly, as she finally caught up with him. 'Here, in Thimphu?'

'Just outside Thimphu,' Daniel replied briefly. 'She has a house up in the hills.'

'Only a house?' said Josie, with a touch of disappointment. 'Not a palace?'

For a moment, he almost smiled again. 'Only a house,' he confirmed.

They got into the car that was waiting outside. It whisked them through Thimphu and then began to climb up a narrow, steep road.

Josie, who was sitting in the back with Daniel and feeling unexpectedly nervous, suddenly clutched at his hand.

'I'm not *dressed* to meet a princess,' she hissed at him. 'You whisked me out so quickly that I didn't have time to change my clothes.'

She was wearing a cotton skirt and matching T-shirt. They were clean, but definitely very casual.

Daniel seemed unconcerned. In fact, he was wearing his usual outfit of jeans and sweatshirt. *Not* the kind of outfits to wear for a royal visit! Josie thought that they looked like a couple of hitch-hikers.

'The princess is quite modern in her outlook,' he told her. 'She won't be concerned about what we're wearing. And would you mind squeezing my hand a little less tightly?'

Highly embarrassed, Josie very quickly let go of it. She hadn't even realised that she was still holding on to it. Don't touch him again, she instructed herself edgily. She definitely didn't want him to get the wrong idea!

The car drew up outside the princess's house, which was set among pleasant gardens. Daniel got out of the car, and Josie followed him as he headed towards a flight of steep steps that led up towards the entrance. At the top of the stairs, Josie could see someone waiting for them.

'Is that the princess?' she whispered to him.

'I should think so,' he replied.

'Don't you *know*?' she said with surprise. 'I mean, you've met her, haven't you? You must know what she looks like!'

'No, I've never met her,' Daniel said, to her astonishment.

'But you kept talking as if you knew her!' she said indignantly. 'All the way to Bhutan, you've rattled on about this princess. And now you're telling me that you haven't even met her!'

'Don't get over-excited,' Daniel said, in that calm voice that she was beginning to find more than a little irritating. 'And I never said that I'd met the princess. Only that she was helping to arrange this trip for us.'

'Why should she do that, if she doesn't even know you?' demanded Josie.

'I haven't met the princess, but I did meet her husband, in London. I talked to him about the documentary I was hoping to make, and he was very interested. He offered to help cut through all the red tape involved in getting to Bhutan, and to give me assistance when I was actually here. Now, will you keep your voice down? I'd rather not have a stand-up argument in front of the princess.'

They were almost at the top of the steps now. Josie looked up, and saw that the princess was wearing the brightly coloured traditional dress of Bhutan, pinned on each shoulder with silver brooches. Her hair was short and dark, and she had smiling, intelligent eyes.

Josie suddenly panicked. 'Do I curtsy?' she muttered to Daniel, under her breath.

'That's entirely up to you,' he replied. 'It would certainly be the polite thing to do, but it isn't compulsory.'

In the end, Josie gave a sort of bob as they approached the princess, balancing rather precariously on the narrow step of the stairs. It was about the nearest to a curtsy that she could come, not having had a great deal of practice in such things.

'Please come in,' said the princess, in excellent English.

She led them into a drawing-room, which had large windows that overlooked the valley and the city of Thimphu. Servants brought in bowls of butter tea and plates of crisped rice, and the princess and Daniel talked for a while about the documentary he was hoping to make.

Josie began to feel rather out of it. She wasn't sorry she had come, though. This might not be a palace, but it was definitely a royal residence, and it was probably the first and last time in her life that she would set foot in such a place.

'And are you enjoying your visit to Bhutan?' asked the princess, suddenly turning to her.

'Oh—yes,' said Josie, in a flustered voice. 'Although I haven't seen very much of your country yet, of course.'

'You will see much more of it if you continue working for Mr Hayden,' the princess told her. 'However, this isn't a good time of the year for travelling,' she warned, her dark gaze moving back to Daniel. 'This is the monsoon season. You may find some of the roads blocked by landslides.'

'I know that,' replied Daniel, 'but this was the only free slot in my schedule. There was no other time I could come to Bhutan. But if we decide to go ahead with the documentary, we'll be filming during the dry season. Right now, though, I want to have a good look around, decide where I want to film, and draw up a rough working schedule.'

'I have arranged transport for you, and of course I will give you every assistance I can,' said the princess. She stood up, and Josie and Daniel did likewise. 'I wish you every luck with your project,' she said.

That obviously signalled the end of their audience with her. They left the tranquil, sunlit drawing-room, went back down the long flight of steps and got into the car.

'Everything seems to be going very well so far,' remarked Daniel, with some satisfaction.

Josie wasn't altogether sure that she agreed with that. From his point of view, she supposed that things *were* going well. She kept getting definite twinges of unease, though. She didn't know why; there didn't seem any reason for them, but they were definitely

there, running through her nervous system and making
her feel uncharacteristically on edge.

Well, you've got a choice, she reminded herself. You
can carry on into the wilds of Bhutan, with Daniel,
or you can go straight back to Calcutta, and, from
there, home to England. No one's forcing you to go
anywhere with this man.

Then she gave a small sigh. She didn't really have
a choice at all. Her own stubbornness wouldn't let her
turn back so soon, especially when there was so much
of Bhutan that she hadn't yet seen.

Josie decided to ignore her twitching nerve-ends,
work hard over the next few days, enjoy this visit to
Bhutan, and, whenever it was possible, to keep a very
safe distance between herself and Daniel Hayden!

CHAPTER FOUR

THE next morning, Josie went down very early to breakfast. She intended to eat quickly, and then go out and see something of Thimphu before Daniel was even up.

She was a little annoyed, therefore, to find him already sitting in the dining-room as she walked in.

'Are you always up this early?' she asked.

'I don't usually sleep very much,' he replied.

'Why?' she enquired flippantly. 'Guilty conscience?'

He shot a quick, hard look at her, which made her promptly shut up. This man didn't seem to appreciate humour, she reminded herself. In future, she would remember to avoid jokes, even very feeble ones.

'Well, what's the programme for today?' she asked, deciding this would be a good time to change the subject.

'This morning, we'll visit the Tashicho Dzong. The princess has given us special permission to see inside.'

At that, Josie brightened up. She was longing to see inside the great fortress-cum-monastery that dominated the tiny city of Thimphu.

'This afternoon,' continued Daniel, 'I've some people to see, officials who'll be involved in all the paperwork that I'll have to get through, if I decide to go ahead with the documentary. Then, tomorrow, we'll leave Thimphu and head eastwards.'

Josie quickly finished her breakfast. If they were going to have just one day in Thimphu, then she wanted to make the most of it.

They walked to the Tashicho Dzong, and Josie had to admit that she felt slightly awestruck as she stood under its huge, white, buttressed walls. Daniel had a camera slung over his shoulder, and took several shots of the outside. Then they went up a great flight of stone steps that led them into a massive courtyard.

In the centre of the courtyard was a tall tower, and at the far end a row of columns in front of a white-washed wall painted with huge murals. Gold and scarlet dragons twisted round the top of the columns, and a pair of massive beaten copper doors stood open behind them. Beyond them was a darkened room, from which strange music was coming.

Josie found she was chewing her lip rather nervously. 'Should we go any further?' she whispered.

'I don't see why not,' replied Daniel, in a practical voice. 'Why are you whispering?'

'I don't know,' she admitted. 'There's something about this place—it's got a special kind of atmosphere. Can't you feel it?'

But if he could, he certainly wasn't going to admit it. Instead, he took some more photos, and then walked towards the huge copper doors.

Josie followed him, but more slowly. The sun glinted down on Daniel's head, illuminating his gold-brown hair and turning it into a bright halo. His shoulders seemed even broader than usual, and she realised that his hands, hanging loose by his sides, had supple, well-shaped fingers. She had never noticed that before.

A little disturbed, she wrenched her gaze away from him and instead looked ahead. She could see now that beyond the great copper doors lay a huge hall. The walls had been fitted with shelves, from floor to ceiling, and on the shelves stood thousands of gold figures of Buddha, glinting in the shadows. At the back of the hall was another, very much larger figure of Buddha, and in the centre aisle were rows of red-robed monks.

It was the monks who were producing the strange music that drifted out of the hall. They were playing drums, decorated with more dragons, bells, flutes and cymbals.

Josie stood listening, entranced. The music was quite alien to her Western ears, but at the same time something inside her responded to it. She was aware that Daniel was standing just as silently and as still. Perhaps he, too, had finally been affected by the haunting atmosphere of this place.

After what seemed to Josie like a very long time, they left the hall and walked back to the courtyard, walking very quietly so as not to disturb the monks. The sunlight seemed very bright after the darkness of the hall, and she blinked rather dazedly. As her eyes slowly adjusted to the light, she found that Daniel was standing a little way away from her, but looking at her.

They hadn't spoken to each other for some time, and they didn't say anything now. His gold-brown eyes seemed to have lost some of their indifference, though. In fact, he was looking at her as if he were really seeing her for the very first time. Noticing details, instead of letting his gaze flicker over her without registering any more than a general impression.

He stared at the bright gold of her hair. Then his gaze rested very briefly on the dark blue of her eyes. Finally, he looked away again, and Josie had the strange impression that he was somehow disturbed.

'What is it?' she said a little hesitantly.

'Nothing,' he said abruptly. He seemed to gather himself together. 'Nothing at all.' He busied himself with the camera, taking several shots, as if he needed to find something to do with his hands. When he had finished, he slung the camera back over his shoulder. 'I've seen enough of this place. If you want to, though, you can stay on for a while and take a longer look around.'

Josie had the distinct impression that he wanted her to do precisely that. In fact, she would have quite liked to have stayed here for a couple more hours. It was one of the most fascinating places she had ever been in, but she didn't think she wanted to stay on her own. Anyway, she was suddenly more interested in sticking close to Daniel. Something about his odd change of attitude had aroused her curiosity.

'No, I'll come with you,' she told him.

He growled something incomprehensible under his breath. Then he strode off towards the gate, leaving her to keep up with his fast pace as best she could.

He didn't say a single word during the walk back to the hotel. Nor did he look at her. By now, Josie was beginning to wish that she *had* stayed at the Tashicho Dzong. He certainly wasn't much fun to be with when he was in this sort of mood!

Then she realised that that was what was odd about this situation. Daniel Hayden wasn't a man who had moods. Oh, he showed brief flashes of temper very occasionally, but mostly he seemed to show a deliberately bland face to the world. Something had happened to change that, though, and Josie found herself wondering what it was.

When they arrived back at the hotel, he turned to her. 'I'm going up to shower and change,' he said rather abruptly. 'Then I'll be out for the rest of the afternoon.'

'Aren't you going to have any lunch?' she asked, surprised.

'I'm not hungry.'

'Well, what am I meant to do, while you're out?'

'Whatever you want,' he told her, in the same clipped tones.

'I suppose I could go sightseeing. Or do you want me to stay here and make notes?'

'On what?'

'Well—anything that I think might be useful to you.'

He didn't seem to want to look directly at her. 'There's no need to make notes. I've taken photos of everything in Thimphu that interests me.'

'The Tashicho Dzong was a fascinating place, wasn't it?' Josie said in a slightly dreamy voice. 'I've never been anywhere quite like it. And it had such a strange atmosphere. Very peaceful, very silent—almost enchanted.'

'I didn't notice anything,' Daniel said flatly. 'It was an interesting old building, that was all.'

Josie was absolutely certain that he was lying. She had never before seen him look quite the way he had, standing in that great courtyard. He had looked—almost human, she concluded. Although the effect that the Tashicho Dzong had had on him obviously hadn't lasted!

'Anyone who isn't impressed by the Tashicho Dzong obviously hasn't got a soul,' she teased him lightly.

He gave a grim little half-smile. 'You're probably right. And perhaps it would be as well if you remembered that, in the future.'

With that, he swung away from her and strode off. Josie stared after him, until he had disappeared from sight. He was a very strange man! she decided with a grimace. And one whom it would be almost impossible to get to know.

Not that she *wanted* to get to know him, she assured herself hurriedly. Daniel Hayden was her employer, and nothing more.

She told herself that twice, to make very sure that she didn't forget it. Then she went up to shower and change, before lunch.

After she had eaten, she wondered how she should spend the free afternoon that stretched before her. Return to the Tashicho Dzong, for a more leisurely look around? But she already knew that she didn't really want to go back there. She might start remembering the way Daniel had looked at her as they had stood in that sunlit courtyard, and that was something that she had already decided she wanted to forget.

In the end, she decided just to wander around Thimphu and look at the shops. The main street was lined with them, although they were certainly nothing like the stores she was used to back home! The interiors were dark and musty, and many of them gave off some very strange smells. A lot sold food: rice and flour, dried fish and cheese, onions, chillis, and eggs. Others were stacked with brightly coloured silks and wool, jewellery, delicately carved boxes and bamboo handicrafts.

In the end, after much deliberation, she bought a silver bracelet with a dragon patterned on it. The symbol of the dragon seemed to be everywhere in Bhutan, the Land of the Thunder Dragon. Josie almost felt as if she wouldn't be too surprised to meet one face to face.

Or perhaps she already had! she told herself with a wry grin. She had the feeling that Daniel Hayden wasn't quite the cool man that she had first thought him to be. Perhaps he was quite capable of breathing fire if he was ever really aroused over something!

Almost as if thinking about him had somehow conjured him up, Josie walked round a corner and found herself face to face with Daniel Hayden.

She gulped very hard. To be suddenly confronted with him like this was somehow very disconcerting.

'I thought . . .' Her voice had a distinct croak in it, and, after clearing her throat, she tried again. 'I thought you were going to be tied up all afternoon with business meetings?'

'Everything went a lot more smoothly than I'd expected,' he said briefly. 'The meetings took only a short time.'

She had the feeling that he wasn't particularly pleased to see her. She didn't know why, though. As far as she knew, she hadn't done anything to provoke this sort of reaction from him.

'What are you doing in this part of Thimphu?' she asked, trying to keep the conversation on a fairly friendly level.

'I'm looking for a bar,' Daniel replied, his gold-brown eyes meeting hers starkly, as if challenging her to make some disapproving comment.

Josie had no intention of doing any such thing. If, for some reason that he obviously wasn't going to explain to her, he needed a drink, then it was no business of hers.

'There's a bar at the end of the street,' she told him, in a rather flat voice.

As he wheeled round and walked off in that direction, she found herself following him. She was quite certain that it wasn't a good idea, but at the same time she didn't think that he ought to be left on his own while he was in this kind of mood.

Halfway down the street, he seemed to realise that she was just behind him. He abruptly stopped, and turned back to face her.

'Go back to the hotel,' he ordered.

'I'd sooner come with you.' There was a stubborn note in her voice that her family and friends would certainly have recognised. 'I've never been inside a Bhutanese bar. In fact, I'm surprised that they have bars,' she rattled on brightly, ignoring the black frown that was gathering behind his eyes. 'This is a very religious country, isn't it? Aren't intoxicants of any kind frowned on?'

'Officially, yes, but Bhutan still produces an amazing amount of different drinks.'

'And do you intend to sample all of them in one afternoon?' Josie asked boldly.

She was amazed that she had had the nerve to ask him such a thing, especially when his face warned her that he was in no mood for this kind of conversation.

He kept control of his temper, though. She was beginning to realise that it would take a great deal to make him lose that self-control that he obviously prized so highly.

'I think that my drinking habits are my affair,' he informed her in a cold tone. 'As I remember, I employed you as a personal assistant, not a babysitter.'

'Yes, you did,' she agreed. 'But, since we're travelling together, anything you do affects me. And your aunt Katherine seemed to think that you might have a drinking problem.'

The words popped out before she could stop them, and she instantly regretted them. She regretted it even more when she saw the expression that spread over Daniel Hayden's face.

'My problem isn't alcohol,' he said in a voice that was all the more dangerous because it was so unnaturally controlled. 'In fact, right now my main problem seems to be an employee who can't keep her nose out of my affairs!'

He strode off again, and Josie stared after him, her eyebrows drawing together in a frustrated frown. For some reason, she always seemed to say the wrong thing to this man.

'What do I do now?' she muttered to herself, under her breath. 'Go back to the hotel? Try and forget any of this happened?'

She decided that would be the sensible thing to do. So why, a few seconds later, did she begin to march off down the street after Daniel?

If you're going to work closely with him over the next few days, then you need to know more about him, she reasoned with herself. You need to get to know his moods, and find out how to cope with them.

Or perhaps the real reason she was following him was quite simple. She was increasingly curious about this man, and what made him tick.

Of course, she wasn't interested in him *personally*, she assured herself. There was nothing in the least romantic in this growing curiosity. He was like a complicated puzzle that she wanted to solve.

Daniel had disappeared into the bar by now, and Josie marched in after him. Inside, it was dark, and the walls were covered with gaudy posters advertising Indian films.

He turned round and shot a black look at her as she walked over to him. 'Why do you keep following me?'

Josie shrugged. 'You're the only person I know in Bhutan. Unless I stick with you, I'll be completely on my own.'

'You don't strike me as the type who gets nervous if you have to spend a couple of hours by yourself.'

She shrugged. 'I've spent the whole afternoon by myself. The novelty's beginning to wear off. Anyway, I've forgotten how to get back to the hotel. Unless I stay close to you, I'll get completely lost.'

'No one can get lost in Thimphu. It's too small.'

Josie gave him a bright smile. 'I still think I'll stick close. I feel safer with someone I know.'

His eyes took on a strange gleam. 'You feel safe with me?'

'Yes,' she said very firmly, as if she needed to convince herself, as well as him.

His mouth curled into a totally unexpected half-smile; a smile that did not quite reach his eyes. Then it quickly faded away again.

'Why have you really followed me into this bar?'

Since she didn't actually know the answer to that question, she gave a small shrug of her shoulders. 'Perhaps I'm like you. I want a drink.'

'It isn't because my aunt Katherine told you to watch me, in case I wanted too many drinks?'

'Your aunt told me very little about you,' Josie said, after a short pause.

'A little while ago, you said that she thought I might have a drinking problem.' His eyes bored into her as he spoke, making her shift around rather restlessly on the hard wooden stool she was sitting on.

'She didn't actually *say* that,' she admitted, rather uncomfortably. 'It was just something I guessed, from the general drift of the conversation.'

'You're a very perceptive girl,' Daniel remarked, in a not particularly pleasant voice. 'And I suppose you're worried, in case you're setting off into the wilds of Bhutan with a confirmed alcoholic?'

'No, of course not,' she said hurriedly, but somehow there wasn't a great deal of conviction in her voice.

His gold-brown eyes fixed on her. 'There was a time when I came close to having a problem with drink. It never developed into anything serious, and it certainly isn't a problem any more. Does that satisfy you?'

'Yes,' she mumbled.

'Good. In that case, I'll now have a drink—*one* drink,' he added, in a voice edged with sarcasm. 'And then we'll return to the hotel.'

'I think I'll have one, as well,' Josie said, with a shaky sigh. She didn't usually drink—she didn't actually like alcohol very much—but she definitely felt as if she needed one right now!

'What do you want?'

'The same as you, I suppose. What are you having?'

'A locally produced whisky. It's called Bhutan Mist.'

'Bhutan Mist?' she echoed disbelievingly.

'It's supposed to be very good.' For the first time in ages, he seemed to relax just a fraction. 'If you don't fancy that, there are several other drinks you can try. How about Dragon Rum?'

'More dragons!' she said a little gloomily. 'I'm beginning to think the place is overrun with them. All right, I'll try the Dragon Rum.'

Daniel ordered the drinks, and emptied his own glass in a couple of practised swallows. 'Not bad,' he said, surprised. 'Aren't you going to try yours?'

She lifted her own glass, hesitated a trifle nervously, and then took a small sip. Almost immediately, she closed her eyes.

'What's it like?' enquired Daniel, with some interest.

'Don't ask,' she answered faintly. She pushed the glass away and gave a small shudder.

'How about some Bhutan Mist, to take the taste away?' suggested Daniel slyly.

'I think I've had quite enough of Bhutanese bars,' she said with some feeling. 'I'd like to go back to the hotel, please.'

Outside, they found that the sky had grown ominously dark. The heavy monsoon rain fell mostly during the late afternoon and early evening, and it looked as if it was about to descend on them at any moment.

'Let's get moving,' said Daniel, and Josie didn't stop to argue with him.

They were barely halfway along the street when the first drops of rain began to fall. A minute later, it was streaming down in great sheets. After that, there was no point in hurrying. They were already soaked right through to the skin. They couldn't possibly get any wetter.

'This definitely isn't a good time to come to this part of the world,' Josie commented, shaking her dripping hair and wiping the streaming rain out of her eyes.

'I didn't have much choice,' Daniel replied. 'I've a very full schedule this year. This was the only time I could come. What about you, though? You could have booked your holiday at some other time, couldn't you?'

'It wasn't a holiday, it was a honeymoon,' she reminded him. 'And when I originally picked a date for the wedding I wasn't thinking about whether or not it was the time of the monsoons! Derek didn't come up with the idea of a honeymoon in Bhutan until some time later.'

It was funny, but there was no note of bitterness in her voice when she spoke about the honeymoon, and Derek. She didn't even feel particularly angry any more. Or perhaps she was just too wet to feel anything! she told herself wryly.

They finally squelched into the hotel, leaving small puddles of water behind them as they headed towards the stairs. Before they reached them, though, the manager came bustling towards them, a very worried expression on his face.

'May I please have a word with you, sir?' he said. As Daniel nodded, he edged him to one side and then began talking to him in a rapid, anxious voice.

Josie decided that she might as well go on up to her room. Whatever the manager wanted to speak to Daniel about so urgently, it didn't concern her.

She was just starting up the stairs when the manager glanced over at her. 'Please, madam, would you mind waiting?' Then he resumed his conversation with Daniel, his hands moving expressively now as the words kept pouring out.

Josie was getting rather fed up with this. Water was still dripping off her, and her clothes were clinging clammily to her skin. She wanted to strip off, dry herself, and get into some fresh clothes.

'How much longer is this going to take?' she muttered, as the conversation between Daniel and the manager seemed to go on and on.

In the end, she decided she had waited long enough. She was going up to her room right now, and if the manager didn't like it, then too bad!

Just then, though, Daniel nodded to the manager, who looked thoroughly relieved, as if some very satisfactory agreement had just been reached.

'What on earth was that all about?' she asked, as Daniel walked over to rejoin her. 'No, don't tell me,' she added a little crossly. 'I'm not interested. I just want to get upstairs and into some dry clothes.'

'You should be interested,' Daniel told her. 'The manager wants to ask a very big favour of both of us.'

'Then why didn't he include me in the conversation?' demanded Josie, becoming even more annoyed.

Daniel's eyes glinted. 'He thought the matter was a little—delicate. That was why he wanted to speak to me about it first.'

Her own gaze began to grow wary. 'Delicate?' she echoed. 'What do you mean, delicate?'

'He's got a problem. A party of trekkers have returned a day earlier than expected. That means he doesn't have enough rooms for them all.'

'Well, I don't see what that's got to do with us...' began Josie. Then her eyes narrowed. 'Wait a minute,' she said suspiciously. 'Are you trying to tell me...?'

'I think you're beginning to get the gist of it,' said Daniel, a half-smile touching the corners of his mouth. 'The manager was very politely trying to find out just how friendly we were.'

'I hope you told him that we weren't friends at all,' she said fiercely. Then she went a little red as she realised just how rude that sounded. 'I didn't mean it quite like that,' she muttered.

'I know you didn't,' he said in an unperturbed voice. 'And I explained that we were simply business colleagues. I also told him that it wouldn't cause us any problems if we had to share a room for one night.'

'You told him *what*?' she yelped.

He looked as if his patience was finally beginning to wear a little thin. 'We've been through all this before,' he reminded her. 'I warned you that we might find ourselves in a situation where there would be only one room available. If I remember rightly, you agreed that it wouldn't be a problem.'

Josie couldn't recall agreeing to any such thing. 'The way *I* remember it, you said that this situation might arise if we found ourselves in a really out-of-the-way spot, where the accommodation was very limited. Right now, we're in a hotel in the middle of Thimphu, so I hardly think those conditions apply!'

To her surprise, he didn't retaliate with increased impatience. Instead, he simply shrugged. 'I should have known you'd react rather childishly to this. It would be very easy for us to share a room tonight and let the manager have the extra free room that he needs, but if you don't trust me—or yourself—then there's no point in arguing about it any further. I'll tell the manager that the arrangement's off.'

Josie glared at him. It definitely annoyed her, his implication that it was herself she didn't trust, not him. And she hated to be accused of being immature.

'I didn't say I wouldn't agree to share. It's just that I'd like to have been included in the discussion before this whole thing was agreed!'

'I've already explained that,' Daniel said calmly. 'The manager wasn't sure of our relationship. He didn't want to cause you any embarrassment by suggesting something that you might find deeply offensive.'

'I don't get embarrassed that easily.'

The corners of his mouth curled into another very faint smile. 'I know that, but the manager didn't. Are you happy to share my room, then? It's got twin beds, so there won't even be any arguments over who's going to sleep in the chair.'

Josie definitely *wasn't* happy, but she didn't quite see how she could get out of it. Anyway, she supposed it would be good practice, in case a similar situation arose once they had left Thimphu.

'You'd better go and tell the manager to move my things into your room,' she muttered very reluctantly.

'I've already told him,' he said in an unruffled tone.

'You've what?' She threw a black look at him. 'You seem to have assumed an awful lot!'

'I simply assumed that you'd behave in an adult and reasonable manner.' His eyes became a fraction cooler. 'I think that childishness is a very unattractive trait in both men and women.'

Josie's reply was very rude, but she kept her voice low enough so that he couldn't hear it. She didn't like this situation, not at all, but she seemed to have been very cleverly edged into a corner that she simply couldn't get out of. At least, not without throwing the kind of scene that would have Daniel Hayden labelling her as totally immature.

All the same, she felt distinctly uneasy as she followed him up the stairs, and even more edgy as they went into his room. Her bags were already standing by one of the beds, and to try and cover up her nervousness she went over and opened one of her cases.

After pulling out jeans and a T-shirt, she straightened up again.

'I'm going to have a shower,' she said, a little defiantly.

'Throw me out a towel, will you?' he asked casually, as she went into the bathroom. 'I'll just dry myself, and put on clean clothes, before dinner.'

She chucked out a towel, and then hurriedly closed the bathroom door behind her. It felt very odd to be sharing a room with him. She didn't know why it felt so odd—only that all her nerve-ends seemed to be gently vibrating.

She felt slightly better after she had showered, dried herself, and wriggled into dry clothes. Her hair was still damp, but she ran her fingers through it and then left it to dry naturally, in a tousle of blonde curls.

When she finally left the bathroom, she was relieved to find that Daniel was dressed, and obviously ready to go down to dinner. She had been afraid that she might come out and find him half naked, which would have been highly embarrassing! At least, *she* would have found it embarrassing. She had the feeling that Daniel probably wouldn't have turned a hair!

The food was excellent that evening, but for some reason Josie didn't enjoy it. She didn't even feel particularly hungry. Of course, it wasn't because she was nervous, she assured herself several times. It was probably tiredness. It had been a long day, and she was ready for bed.

As soon as she said that last word to herself, she wished that she hadn't. It conjured up pictures of those twin beds waiting for them, much closer together than she would have liked.

She was fervently beginning to wish that she hadn't let him talk her into this situation. How had it happened? She wasn't quite sure. All she knew was that he had a habit of getting his own way, once he had set his mind to something.

Her eyes were feeling very heavy now. It was hot in the dining-room, and rather stuffy. A minute later, she yawned.

'Tired?' asked Daniel.

'Oh—no,' she said hastily. She didn't want him suggesting that they went up to bed. Not yet, anyway. She just didn't feel ready for it. 'Are we still leaving Thimphu in the morning?' she asked, making a rather obvious attempt to change the subject.

He nodded. 'And fairly early, so don't make any plans for lying in bed late.'

She had no intention of doing that. In fact, she was going to be out of that bed as soon as her eyes opened!

Daniel glanced at his watch. 'Perhaps it would be a good idea to have an early night.'

'Oh—I never go to bed very early,' she said in rather a rush. 'Anyway, doesn't the hotel provide some kind of entertainment in the evening? Or perhaps there's somewhere else we could go?'

'Bhutan isn't noted for its nightlife,' he said drily. 'And there's a very good reason for that. It doesn't have any.'

'Oh,' she said, in a deflated tone.

'So, we might as well go up to bed,' he added.

Josie wished that he wouldn't keep saying the word 'bed'. There was nothing in the least suggestive about his tone of voice when he said it, but that didn't stop tiny shivers from skittering over her skin every time she heard it.

His gold-brown eyes looked distinctly amused now. She had the feeling that he knew *exactly* how she was feeling—and that he was finding it highly entertaining.

In the end, though, he seemed to take pity on her. 'You can go up first, if you like,' he offered. 'I'll stay down here for a while longer. That'll give you time to wash, sort out your things, and do whatever else you need to do.'

Josie wasn't going to turn down an offer like that. She scuttled up the stairs, threw off her clothes, wriggled into the most respectable nightdress she had brought with her, and then burrowed under the light coverings on the bed.

All she had to do now was to get to sleep before he came up. That way, there wouldn't be any awkward moments. And in the morning, with luck, she would be up and dressed before he had even opened his eyes.

If she wasn't asleep by the time he came up, then she was definitely going to pretend that she was. Just minutes after clambering into the bed, though, the tiredness that she had been fighting off earlier swept over her again, and she slipped into a deep, genuine sleep.

That meant she didn't see Daniel when he finally came up to their room. Didn't know that he stood looking at her for a few minutes, his gaze resting on the blonde curls that tumbled over the pillow, and on the slim curve of her neck. Didn't know that he gave an odd, self-mocking half-smile, and then took a very cool shower before finally going to bed.

CHAPTER FIVE

JOSIE woke up in the morning, stretched luxuriously, and realised that it was a long time since she had slept that well. Not since Derek's announcement that he was throwing her over for the doe-eyed Fern, in fact.

She gave the pillow a thump, to fluff it up, and thought that she might have another half-hour in bed. Then she wrinkled her nose. She seemed to remember Daniel saying something about an early start, last night.

Suddenly, her dark blue eyes flew wide open. Daniel! She was sharing a room with him! How on earth could she have forgotten something like that?

Her heart thumping edgily, she sat up, clutching the cover very close to her. Then she nervously turned her head, to look at the other bed.

A second later, she let out a huge sigh of relief. It was empty. He was already up.

She wriggled out of bed and headed towards the bathroom. She would have a quick shower and then get dressed before he came back again. He was probably downstairs right now, having an early breakfast.

She hurried through the bathroom door, and cannoned straight into Daniel. A rather strangled yelp escaped her, and not just because he had briefly knocked the breath out of her. He was wearing just a pair of jeans, which meant he was naked from the waist up. For a couple of moments, she had found herself in very close contact with that bare chest, and it had been an unexpectedly unsettling experience.

'I'm—er—that is—I thought you'd——' she gabbled.

'You thought I'd already left the room?' he finished for her, one eyebrow slowly rising. 'Give me another five minutes, and I will be out of here. I think I need to put on a shirt and some shoes before I go down to breakfast, though.'

Her gaze seemed to be drawn back to the broad, tanned expanse of his chest. Josie realised that she was staring at him, and hurriedly looked down. Now, she was looking at his bare feet. Nice feet, for a man, she thought irrelevantly. Well-shaped and strong.

'I'll—er——' She made a big effort to get hold of herself, and tried again. 'I'll use the bathroom, while you finish dressing.'

'That seems like a very satisfactory arrangement,' he said gravely.

She had the feeling that those gold-brown eyes were laughing at her. She couldn't *see* any laughter in them, of course—she was beginning to wonder if anyone had ever seen this man laugh—but she was certain that there was a gleam of amusement lurking in their golden depths.

They seemed to have reached some sort of impasse. He was still blocking the bathroom door, and Josie didn't want to try pushing past him. It would be all too easy to get into an awkward and embarrassing tussle and she didn't think she could cope with it, not this early in the morning.

To her relief, a couple of seconds later he moved smoothly aside. Josie shot into the bathroom, shut the door behind her and then leant against it, her knees feeling ridiculously weak.

This is a really silly way to behave, she lectured herself severely, when she felt slightly more in control of herself again. For heaven's sake, you've seen a bare chest before!

She had the feeling that it wasn't really his semi-nakedness that had disturbed her. That was the trouble. She didn't know quite *what* it was that was beginning to unsettle her so thoroughly.

By the time she had finished dressing, she had managed to push the entire incident to the very back of her mind. There were other things to think about, including the fact that they were very shortly going to be leaving Thimphu, and setting off on an exploration of other parts of Bhutan.

Josie hurried down to the dining-room and forced down a quick breakfast. There was no sign of Daniel, for which she was rather grateful. He must have finished eating, and gone to check the arrangements for their departure.

She had just gulped down a last cup of coffee when he came into the dining-room, looking for her.

'Are you ready to go?' he asked.

He seemed all cool efficiency again now. Quite different from the half-naked man who had confronted her in the bedroom. And not at all like the man she had spent so much time with yesterday, with his changeable moods that had somehow made him seem more human.

Josie followed him out to the lobby, and found that he had already brought down her bags. His own luggage was piled to one side, more bulky than hers because it included his photographic equipment and a large supply of film.

She looked at the luggage and then wrinkled her nose. 'We're going to make fairly slow progress if we've got to haul that lot around with us. And how *are* we going to get around? Is there some kind of bus service?'

'There is, but we don't have to use it,' replied Daniel. 'Take a look outside.'

Josie walked through the lobby and out the front entrance. Then she blinked hard. Standing outside the hotel was a shiny new minibus.

'Is that for us?' she asked at last.

'Courtesy of the Department of Tourism. It seems that they're quite keen on having a documentary made about their country, and they're willing to give us all the help we need.'

'Including a minibus,' said Josie, with a happy grin. She really hadn't been looking forward to bumping around the country in a crowded and probably ancient bus.

'A Land Rover would have been more useful, but, since they've thrown in a lot of supplies that we might need, I'm certainly willing to settle for the minibus,' said Daniel. 'Let's get going.'

They slung their bags in the back, and Josie noticed that it was already packed with sleeping-bags, cooking gear, boxes of food and even a couple of tents.

'There's enough stuff here to last us for a month,' she said a little uneasily. 'Just how long are we going to be travelling around?'

'Only a few days,' he told her. 'I'd have liked longer, but I've got to be back in England by the end of next week.'

Josie immediately felt happier. She could certainly cope with Daniel Hayden for a few more days. No problem, she told herself confidently, as she climbed into the front seat beside him.

Watery sunshine beamed down on them as they left Thimphu. The minibus rattled along briskly, and she found that she was quite looking forward to the trip that lay ahead of them.

They travelled in silence for quite some time. The road climbed up to the pass above Thimphu and then began to wind down the other side in a series of hairpin bends. Cloud wreathed the craggy peaks which reared up on one side of the road, while on the other there was a dizzying drop down to deep gorges. Josie began to chew her lip rather nervously and hoped that Daniel was a good driver, especially as the cloud seemed to be closing in around them more thickly.

'Are you sure we're going the right way?' she asked slightly edgily, at last.

'Yes,' he said calmly.

The minibus whizzed round a tight bend and she briefly closed her eyes.

'Would you mind going a little slower?' she said through gritted teeth.

His foot stayed firmly pressed down on the accelerator. 'We've a fair amount of mileage to cover today. If we don't reach Tongsa by nightfall, we might have to sleep in one of those tents.'

'Well, I'd sooner sleep in a tent than end up at the bottom of one of those gorges,' she retorted.

He almost grinned. 'You don't have much confidence in my driving.'

'That's because I've never been in a car with you before. I didn't know that you turned into a Formula One driver as soon as you got behind the wheel!'

Daniel seemed quite unperturbed by her remarks. He was obviously in one of his very calm moods, when absolutely nothing fazed him. Josie scowled at him and then stared straight ahead of her. If she didn't look down at those gorges, perhaps she could forget they were there!

The cloud gradually began to lift again and patches of blue sky began to appear. Josie could see valleys stretching out ahead of them, enclosed by thickly forested mountainsides, with tantalising glimpses of monasteries, temples and villages. Then the road they were following began to descend into one of the valleys, and she sighed audibly with relief as they left the deep gorges behind them.

The sun was soon blazing out and it began to get very hot. Paddy fields spread out over the floor of the valley, bright green in the dazzling sunshine, and eucalyptus trees grew along the banks of a river which ran parallel with the road.

Early in the afternoon, they rattled through a small village which seemed totally deserted. There were several shops and market stalls, a single petrol pump, but no signs of life.

'If this were America, I think they'd call this a one-horse town,' Josie remarked wryly.

'There doesn't seem much point in stopping and trying to get something to eat here,' agreed Daniel.

She groaned. 'I'm starving! If you don't stop soon, I think I'm going to collapse from lack of food.'

'You're not the type to collapse for any reason,' he said unsympathetically. 'You might look frail and fragile, but underneath you're as strong as a horse.'

'That doesn't sound very complimentary,' Josie said with some annoyance. 'And aren't we *ever* going to eat? It's hours since breakfast.'

Daniel pulled the minibus over to the side of the road. 'There's a picnic hamper in the back,' he said. 'You'd better get it out.'

The hamper had obviously been packed by the hotel. There were rolls, cold meat, fresh fruit and bottles of lemonade.

Josie ate hungrily. 'I suppose I'd better make the most of this,' she said with a grin, as she finally finished. 'It'll probably be rice, rice, and more rice from now on!'

'There are some cans of food in one of the boxes in the back of the minibus,' Daniel told her. 'If we get tired of rice, we can switch to tinned stew, Spam and tuna.'

She pulled a face. 'Thanks, but I think I'll stick to the local food, when we can get it.' She shovelled the remains of their lunch into the picnic hamper, and then strolled down to the river, to rinse her hands and face. When she finally returned, she found that Daniel was sitting with his back propped up comfortably against a tree, his eyes closed.

For a few moments, she just stood there looking at him. It struck her how little she still knew about this man, despite the amount of time they had spent together. Nevertheless, he was beginning to seem very familiar; she could close her eyes, and still easily picture the strong lines of his face, the way his gold-brown hair sprang back from his forehead, and the rare glint that she sometimes caught in his eyes.

Then she realised that those same eyes were now open again; open, and looking directly at her. She felt stupidly confused. She shuffled her feet edgily, and tried to think of something to say that wouldn't sound completely inane.

'I didn't expect to find you asleep,' she muttered at last. 'I thought you were the one who wanted to keep moving?'

'I haven't been asleep,' Daniel said lazily.

'Your eyes were closed!'

'I was simply thinking.'

'About what?' Then Josie realised that she shouldn't have asked that question. It wasn't a good idea to show any interest in what this man was thinking.

He didn't seem to want to answer her, anyway. He gave a non-committal shrug, and appeared rather less relaxed than he had been just a few moments ago.

'I've been doing some thinking, as well,' Josie said, looking down at him. 'I'm beginning to wonder just what I'm doing here.'

His eyebrows lifted slightly. 'I'd have thought that was fairly obvious. You're working as my personal assistant.'

'That's the point,' she retorted. 'I'm *not* working. I haven't done anything since we arrived in Bhutan, except for some sightseeing. I don't think that you actually need an assistant.'

'I could probably have managed on my own,' he agreed, in an untroubled voice. 'But I'm hoping that this trip will be more productive with you around. I told you, I want you to look at the country from the female point of view, and then give me any ideas and impressions you pick up.'

'The "female input"?' she said with a grimace.

'Precisely. I usually rely on my permanent assistant, Margaret, to give me a different slant on things and provide me with fresh ideas. Since she's back in England with a broken leg, I looked around to see if there was anyone who could temporarily take her place. You turned up out of the blue, and seemed like the type of person who was capable of looking at things in an original way. That's a talent that's a lot rarer than you might think.'

'You offered me the job almost before you knew me,' Josie pointed out. 'How did you know I was the right sort of person?'

He shrugged. 'I took a chance. And, even if it doesn't work out, it'll still be useful having you around. I want to know how a woman can cope with this trip. A couple of my film crew are women.' He gave a sly grin. 'I'm an equal opportunities employer. And, before I bring them all the way out here to Bhutan, I need to know that the trip won't be too rough on them.'

At that, Josie really began to glare at him. 'In other words, I'm a guinea-pig! If I don't fall over a gorge, catch some really awful Bhutanese virus or collapse with exhaustion after you've dragged me right round the country, then you'll know it's safe to bring your female members of staff out here!'

'That's about it,' said Daniel, in an unperturbed voice.

Her glare deepened. 'If you'd told me all this back in Calcutta, I'd probably never have come.'

'I know. That's why I haven't told you until now.'
His gold-brown eyes glinted. 'Do you want to resign?'

'And if I said yes, what would you do?' she demanded. 'Leave me here, to hitch-hike my way back to Calcutta?'

'Probably,' he said calmly. 'I'm certainly not volunteering to take you back there in person.'

'You've used me—and you've broken your promise,' she accused.

'I don't really see it that way. You're getting a chance to see parts of Bhutan that you wouldn't have seen if you'd stayed with that package tour, and you're even getting paid for it. I think you've done rather well out of our arrangement.'

Josie was quite speechless. Really, the man was completely impossible! And totally self-centred. He didn't care about anything except using people and getting his own way.

'If I had any sense, I'd walk out on you right here and now,' she informed him hotly.

'What's stopping you?' he asked, not sounding in the least worried by her threat.

'Well, it might just be the fact that there isn't anywhere I *can* walk to,' she said sarcastically. 'You made sure that we were in the middle of nowhere before you told me all this.'

'There's a village just a little way back down the road,' he reminded her.

'Oh, yes, the one-horse town—I'm sure they've got a whole fleet of taxis, just waiting to take me back to Thimphu! I can't even hitch-hike,' she said in exasperation. 'We haven't passed a single car all morning. I haven't even seen a yak that I could flag down and hitch a lift on!'

At that, Daniel actually smiled. She was so astonished to see a full, genuine smile on his face that for
a few moments she almost forgot how angry she was.

'Why don't you get back into the minibus, and we'll
just carry on?' he suggested, still looking amused.

'Just like that?'

'I don't see why not. Anyway, as you said,' Daniel
reminded her, 'you don't really have any alternative.'

Josie muttered balefully under her breath as she
clambered back into the minibus. This man hadn't
been very truthful with her, and she didn't like that.
And now she was stuck here with him, on a road that
seemed to be going nowhere, and she didn't like *that*,
either. On top of that, she wasn't sure she believed
any of the reasons he had so far given her for bringing
her to Bhutan.

So, what was she doing getting back into this
minibus with him? She was doing the only thing she
could do, she told herself with a scowl. There was no
way she could walk out on him, and he knew that.
She might be stubbornly independent, but she wasn't
stupid. She knew perfectly well that no girl in her right
mind should travel around a strange country on her
own. And that meant she was going to have to stick
with Daniel Hayden until he finally put her on the
plane back to Calcutta.

Daniel climbed in beside her, started up the engine,
and the minibus rattled off. The road wound upwards, dropped down into another valley that was
heavy with heat, and then began to climb back into
the hills. Josie didn't say a single word. She knew that
Daniel had glanced at her a couple of times, but she
kept her eyes fixed firmly ahead. She wasn't sulking,

she told herself firmly. She just didn't want to see or speak to him at the moment!

The clouds began to close in again and the sun disappeared from sight. She guessed that it would soon start raining, but didn't mind too much. A damp, heavy downpour would just about match her mood.

The roads were beginning to get rather hair-raising again. There was a high cliff on the left-hand side, and a sheer drop on the right. Josie just hoped that they didn't suddenly meet a very large truck coming in the other direction!

Then they turned a corner, and Daniel immediately slammed on the brakes. The road ahead of them seemed to have disappeared under a large heap of rubble.

'What's happened?' she asked with a gulp, as the minibus slewed to a halt.

'A landslide,' replied Daniel briefly. 'Part of the cliff has fallen down. It often happens during the rainy season.'

'What do we do now?'

'Try and clear it.'

'By ourselves?' she squeaked.

'Do you see anyone else around who's likely to give us a hand?'

'Perhaps if we wait someone will come along and help,' she suggested.

'On the other hand, we could sit here for the rest of the day and all of the night without seeing a single soul,' Daniel pointed out. 'Do you want to spend the night in the minibus?'

Josie definitely didn't. It was too cramped—they would be far too close together.

'Let's start digging,' she said hurriedly. 'What do we use? Our bare hands?'

'There are a couple of spades in the back,' he told her. 'They were probably put there in case we ran into a problem like this. We might have to shift some of it by hand, though. Some of those rocks are too large to shovel away.'

Josie collected a spade without much enthusiasm, trudged over to the pile of mud and rocks, and then began to dig. Luckily, it wasn't a major landslide. There was just enough mud and rubble to stop the minibus passing.

After she had been digging for only a few minutes, she felt a few drops of rain hitting her face.

'Oh, great!' she muttered. 'Just to make things really fun, we're going to get soaking wet.'

In no time at all, the rain was whooshing down in great sheets. The mud she was trying to dig was almost liquid now, and she was steadily getting more and more filthy.

'How are you doing?' asked Daniel, splashing over to her.

'I'm doing really well,' she told him, her dark blue eyes glaring at him. 'I'm soaked through, plastered in mud, and my back aches from digging. I haven't had such a good time since I had a really bad dose of the flu!'

'Just keep digging,' he said, with a grin. 'I'll try and shift some of the larger rocks. Another half-hour of hard work, and I reckon we should be able to get through.'

'That's the second time you've smiled today,' she said with some amazement. 'Do you only grin when everything's going totally wrong?'

'This is only a minor hitch, not a major disaster,' he told her.

Rain streamed down Josie's face, plastered her hair to her head, and soaked through every inch of her clothing.

'Well, this seems fairly disastrous to me!' she told him with a black scowl. In a thoroughly bad temper, she kicked at a nearby chunk of rock. She missed, and her feet slid around in the slippery dirt. Her arms waved a little frantically in the air, and a second later she sat down hard in the wet, oozy mud.

She could feel it gurgling up the legs of her jeans and dripping into her shoes. The rain kept streaming down on her head and she gave a great yell of temper and frustration.

Daniel simply stood there looking at her for a few seconds. Then he laughed.

Josie couldn't believe it. She stared up at him, her dark blue eyes beginning to blaze. Then she grabbed hold of a nearby lump of mud and threw it at him.

'It isn't funny!' she roared. 'None of this is funny. How *dare* you laugh at me?'

He sobered up just a little, but his mouth still curled upwards at the corners and his gold-brown eyes danced with an unfamiliar brightness.

'I'm sorry,' he said, but to Josie he didn't sound sorry at all. In fact, she had the feeling that he hadn't enjoyed himself so much for ages.

'I wish I'd never met you,' she shouted at him. 'I certainly wish I'd never come to Bhutan with you!'

He reached out his hand. 'Grab hold, and I'll haul you to your feet.'

Josie ignored him. Instead, she scrambled up by herself, nearly falling down again in the process and only regaining her balance by sheer luck. When she was finally standing up again, rain and mud streaming off her, she turned back to him and fixed him with a fierce glare.

'I don't need your help. I don't even know why I'm here. I'd really like to know the *real* reason why you brought me with you.'

Even through the pouring rain, she could see that his face had altered. He looked at her reflectively for a few moments. Then he said in an unexpectedly low and level voice, 'Perhaps I knew that you were the one person in the world who could make me laugh again.'

That shut her up. She simply didn't know what to say. They stood there staring at each other through the rain for what seemed to Josie like a very long time. Then she dragged her gaze away from his face and edged away from him a little.

'I'm going back to the minibus,' she muttered at last.

He didn't try to stop her. He watched her walk away, and then went back to clearing the landslide.

Once inside the minibus, she slumped down into the seat, water and mud dripping off her. She hardly noticed it any more, though. Instead, she stared out of the window where, through the torrential rain, she could just make out Daniel's tall figure, digging away at the last of the landslide.

Her heart thumped a little faster as he finally strode back to the minibus. 'I think we can get through now,' he said confidently.

He slid into the driver's seat, started up the engine, and drove slowly towards the landslide. The wheels bumped over the debris still scattered across the road, and then slowly began to slide in the thick mud.

Josie swallowed very hard. On the right-hand side of the road was a sheer drop down to the valley below, and the minibus was gently slithering towards the edge.

'I don't think this is a very good idea,' she said in a quavery voice.

'We can make it,' said Daniel, his own tone calm and confident.

She glanced out of the window, and then immediately wished she hadn't. That sheer drop was only inches away! She closed her eyes and said a silent prayer.

The minibus bumped forward a few more feet, slithered in the mud again, and almost came to a complete halt. Then Daniel suddenly revved up the engine, and it rattled across the rest of the landslide at what seemed to Josie a quite suicidal speed. She was absolutely certain they were going to shoot right over the edge and go crashing all the way down to the valley far below them. Instead, the minibus safely reached the road on the far side, and began to trundle along it at a much more sedate speed.

Daniel turned his head and glanced at her. 'You've gone very white,' he remarked.

'That's hardly surprising!' retorted Josie. 'I thought we were going to go flying over the edge. I didn't know that every now and then you get the urge to drive like an absolute maniac!'

'You weren't in any danger,' Daniel said in an unperturbed voice. 'If there had been any risk, I'd have made you get out of the minibus.'

'Then I only imagined that we were just inches from that sheer drop?' she enquired with some sarcasm, the colour slowly beginning to seep back into her face again.

'We were fairly close,' he conceded. 'But there was never any chance that we would go right over.'

'Men!' she muttered. 'You all think you're such wonderful drivers.'

'Do you want to take a turn at the wheel?' he invited.

Josie looked out at the rain-drenched road and the fading light, as early evening approached. 'No,' she said, with a scowl.

They drove on in silence for quite some time. Low cloud obscured the tops of the mountains now, and was threatening to drift down and blot out the road itself.

Daniel gave a small frown. 'I think we'd better try and find somewhere to stop for the night.'

'Shouldn't we be reaching the town of Tongsa fairly soon?' asked Josie. 'That is where we're heading for, isn't it?'

'Yes, it is. But we should actually have reached it some time ago.'

Her dark blue eyes swivelled round to fix on him. 'Are you trying to tell me that we're lost?'

'We may have taken the wrong road somewhere,' he said. He didn't sound in the least worried, which rather annoyed Josie. She felt that getting lost in the middle of Bhutan was definitely something to get edgy over.

'Have you got the slightest idea where we are?' she demanded.

Daniel gave an unconcerned shrug. 'It's difficult to tell, in this rain and mist. The road's fairly good, though, so it must lead somewhere.'

'So we're just going to keep driving?'

'Why not? We're bound to reach a town or village, eventually.'

Josie thought that she would prefer a more positive plan of action. On the other hand, she wasn't sure that there was any reasonable alternative. They could turn back, of course, but it was ages since they had last passed through a village. It would be well into the night before they reached it, and it would also mean negotiating that landslide all over again—and in the dark! She wasn't at all sure that her nerves could stand up to that.

The road they were following led down into a wide valley, and in the centre of the valley were a cluster of houses gathered around a white-walled monastery. Josie let out a sigh of relief. Civilisation!

'The first thing I'm going to do when we've found somewhere to stay is to take a long, hot bath,' she declared. 'I feel absolutely filthy.'

'You are filthy,' Daniel replied cheerfully. 'But I wouldn't count on that bath. We're out in the countryside now. That means no electricity or hot running water. We'll be lucky to find anything except very basic amenities.'

Josie gave a small groan. 'I'm beginning to wish I'd stayed back in Thimphu.'

'No, you don't. Think of all the excitement you'd have missed.'

'Mud, landslides, a near escape from death—I think I can do without that kind of excitement,' she said darkly. Then she peered through the windscreen as they approached the village. 'Where are we going to stay? Have they got some kind of inn?'

'I thought we'd try the monastery,' said Daniel.

'Will they let us in? And even if they do, how are we going to tell them what we want? I don't speak a word of Bhutanese, and I don't suppose you do, either.'

'No more than half a dozen words, and they only cover the basic things like hello and goodbye. I don't think the language will be a problem. If the monks see two tired, dirty travellers turning up on their doorstep, I expect they'll get the message. And we might even be lucky enough to find someone who speaks English. Most educated Bhutanese learn it.'

The minibus came to a halt outside the monastery gates, which stood ajar. There was no sign of any life, though.

'What do we do?' asked Josie. 'Just go in?'

'We might as well,' said Daniel. 'It doesn't look as if anyone's going to come rushing out to meet us.'

Inside the gates was a large and rather overgrown courtyard. A couple of dogs were snoozing in one corner, but apart from that the monastery seemed deserted.

'I don't think there's anyone here,' Josie whispered. She had no idea why she wanted to keep her voice low. Perhaps it had something to do with the rather eerie atmosphere of the place.

Just then, though, a couple of red-robed monks appeared through a doorway at the far side of the courtyard.

'This looks more promising,' remarked Daniel. 'I think they must be the welcoming committee.'

After that, everything seemed to move fairly fast. None of the monks spoke English, but that didn't seem to matter. Josie found herself herded into the monastery, which was dark and rather gloomy inside, and lit only by small flickering lamps. Other monks appeared, to take a look at their unexpected guests, and by the use of much vigorous sign language Daniel managed to make them understand that they would be very grateful for something to eat and a room for the night.

Bowls of tea and plates of rice were produced almost immediately, and the monks didn't seem to mind that their guests were muddy and bedraggled. Then they were taken to a small room at the back of the monastery, and Josie guessed that this was where they were expected to sleep.

Daniel returned to the minibus to fetch sleeping-bags, clean clothes, and a few other things he thought they might need. The room they had been given was almost bare, and the only light came from a tiny, flickering lamp.

One of the things he brought back with him was a battery-operated flash lamp. Josie wasn't sure that she appreciated the brighter light—it simply meant that she could see more clearly what a mess she looked!

To her relief, the monks returned a few minutes later with bowls of water. Then they left them to settle down for the night.

It seemed very quiet in the small room, once the monks had gone. Josie nibbled her lower lip a little uneasily. This was going to be the second night she had shared a room with Daniel Hayden. Last night, she had been asleep and hadn't known much about any of it. Tonight, though, she felt very wide awake, despite the fact that they had been travelling for most of the day.

She wished that she *did* feel tired, and could just flop down on to the sleeping-bag and go straight to sleep. She wished that the monks had given them separate rooms. She wished . . .

She wished she could forget the way Daniel had looked when he had laughed. At the time, she had been very angry. Now, she could remember all too clearly how his eyes had glittered brightly and the taut line of his mouth had relaxed into an unfamiliar softness.

She wished that she understood more about this man, and what went on inside his head. And, most of all, she wished that she liked him a lot less than she did. Because she had the feeling that liking Daniel Hayden was only one step away from something much deeper, and much more dangerous.

CHAPTER SIX

DANIEL began to pull off his clothes.

'What are you doing?' Josie asked nervously.

'I'm going to wash,' he said, unzipping his mud-soaked jeans. 'Is the water hot?'

Josie dipped a finger into the nearest bowl. 'No,' she said, with a grimace. Then, as he peeled off his damp jeans, she rather hurriedly backed towards the door. 'Er—would you like me to wait outside?'

'There doesn't seem a lot of point,' he said with a faint grin. 'We've already seen each other virtually naked. Why suddenly start being prudish?'

She knew that he was right. Yet walking into his hotel room by mistake and inadvertently seeing him naked wasn't quite the same as watching him actually undress!

'Aren't you going to wash?' he asked, as he began to sluice the mud from his arms.

'Oh—yes,' she said in a voice that sounded much edgier than she had intended.

She wriggled out of her grubby T-shirt, dipped a cloth into the cold water and began to scrub herself clean. As soon as her top half was clean, she pulled on a clean T-shirt. Then she wrapped a towel around her waist before wriggling out of her jeans.

She was aware that Daniel was watching her with some amusement. That made the whole awkward procedure even more difficult, and she muttered something very rude under her breath as she clutched at the towel with one hand and tried to wash her grubby legs and feet with the other.

'You'd find it a lot easier if you just let go of that towel and used both hands to wash yourself,' he commented at last.

'Oh, yes, you'd like that, wouldn't you?' she retorted, glaring at him. 'It would give you an uninterrupted view of—of...'

'Of your legs?' Daniel finished for her, his gold-brown eyes gleaming.

He was making her feel as if she was behaving very childishly, and she didn't like that. But, on the other hand, she didn't like him looking at her, either.

'Don't you trust me?' he went on.

'I don't trust any man!' she snapped back at him. 'You're all the same. You say one thing and mean another. You tell someone that you want them, but all you mean is that you want them at that moment. It isn't a lasting thing; next day you want something else—someone else.'

She ran out of breath at that point, and so she shut up. She didn't stop glaring at him, though.

Daniel's own expression had changed by now. 'I think that you're confusing me with someone else,' he warned softly.

'No, I'm not. Men all behave like rats! I don't want anything to do with any of you. I made my mind up about that before I came to Bhutan, and I'm not going to change it.'

'Perhaps I'm not going to *try* and change it,' he said in an even tone.

At that, Josie blinked. That possibility hadn't occurred to her.

'And maybe I have similar views about women,' he went on, in a voice that was now edged with grim undertones. 'Perhaps I believe that they're all scheming and devious, that they always put themselves first and don't give a damn who they hurt or destroy in the process.'

'We're not all like that!' Josie immediately said in a defensive tone. Then she realised that she couldn't have it both ways. She had just insisted that all men were untrustworthy. If she stuck to that viewpoint, then she would have to concede that Daniel had the right to take a similarly low view of women.

'It looks as if we both have a poor view of the opposite sex,' he said at last. The tight line of his mouth relaxed a fraction. 'Perhaps we ought to apply to join one of these monasteries.'

'They won't take me,' said Josie glumly. 'You can't be a female monk.'

'No, you can't,' he agreed, and this time he almost smiled.

Josie began to rub her legs dry and didn't even realise that she was using the towel that she had been trying to keep so carefully wrapped round her waist just a couple of minutes ago.

'Why don't you like women?' she asked at last.

'I didn't say that I didn't like them,' replied Daniel, after a short pause. 'But I would certainly find it very hard to trust one. And I'm not interested in getting involved in any kind of relationship.'

'You still haven't told me why.'

'And I'm not going to. It isn't any of your business.'

At that, she bristled again. Part of her wanted to hit back at him. 'You said just now that you weren't interested in relationships,' she reminded him. 'But back in Thimphu there was quite a lot of talk about casual sex.'

Daniel shrugged. 'I simply wanted to know where you stood on the subject. I'm not interested in relationships, but I am still interested in sex. There was always an outside chance that you would feel the same way.'

'I don't see how you can have sex without some kind of relationship,' Josie argued.

'If you think that way, then you're even more naïve and inexperienced than I supposed,' he said rather brusquely. 'It's very easy to keep the two quite separate.'

For some reason, that last short statement chilled her. 'I don't believe that,' she said in a low voice.

'It's something that you might well find out for yourself in the future, if you're really determined to have nothing more to do with men. Most people need some kind of sexual release. You might find yourself going to bed with someone just to find that release.'

Josie instantly shook her head. 'I won't ever do that.'

His gold-brown eyes rested on hers with a steady thoughtfulness that she found rather unnerving. 'If you were a little less innocent, it might be amusing to prove you wrong. As it is...' he took a slightly deeper breath than usual, and seemed to have to make an effort to keep his tone light '...as it is, we'd better get into our sleeping-bags—our separate sleeping-bags,' he added drily.

Josie hurriedly burrowed into her sleeping-bag, as if it offered some kind of protection against this man who kept saying such unsettling things.

'Goodnight,' she said in a very firm voice, and then she closed her eyes, so that she wouldn't have to look at him any more.

She fell asleep a lot more quickly than she had expected. She must have been more tired than she had thought. In the small hours of the morning, though, she woke up again, and for a few moments she didn't have the slightest idea where she was.

Then it slowly came back to her. She was in a monastery somewhere in the middle of Bhutan. And she was sharing this rather primitive little room with Daniel Hayden.

It was very dark. The flashlight had been turned off, and the lamp that the monks had provided had long ago guttered and died. The only light came from the small window, and, as Josie turned her head in that direction, she saw a black shadow silhouetted against the starlit sky outside.

'Daniel?' she said, her voice coming out a little panicky. 'Is that you?'

'Who else did you think it would be?' he asked with a touch of amusement.

Josie struggled out of the sleeping-bag and groped her way over to the window. There was a half-moon outside, which gave off just enough light for her to see his face as a pale outline in the darkness.

'I don't know who I thought it would be,' she admitted, her voice still rather shaky. 'I woke up and couldn't figure out where I was for a while. It made me feel a bit—well, odd.'

'Are you all right now?'

'Yes—I think so,' she said rather uncertainly. In truth, she still felt slightly disorientated. The unfamiliar room, the darkness, the feeling of being hundreds—thousands—of miles away from everyone and everything she knew. 'Why are you up?' she asked him.

'I had trouble sleeping.'

'Why?'

'You're full of very personal questions, aren't you?'

If there had been more light, he would have seen the faint flush that covered her face. 'You don't have to answer them, if you don't want to,' she mumbled at last.

She sensed, rather than saw, him shrug. 'I don't mind telling you why I'm awake. In fact, I'll do more than that. I'll give you a very good piece of advice. Don't talk too much about sex just before you go to bed. It definitely doesn't help you to sleep.'

'Oh,' she said in a rather startled tone. Then she took a step backwards. 'Oh,' she said again, and her voice was much more guarded this time.

'There's no need to be quite so nervous. I'm not going to pounce on you the moment you get back into your sleeping-bag. Although it's a shame that you're such an old-fashioned girl,' he said, with some regret. 'We could have had quite a lot of fun together.'

At that, Josie bristled. No one had ever called her old-fashioned before, and she didn't like it!

'Just because I don't agree that casual sex is fun, I don't think that makes me old-fashioned,' she said indignantly. 'Plenty of modern girls think the same way as me.'

'It isn't just your attitude to sex. It's the way that you seem to dismiss it as almost irrelevant. It makes me wonder what kind of relationship you had with your fiancé,' he said thoughtfully.

'It was a very warm relationship,' she flashed back at him. 'Very loving.'

Daniel didn't seem impressed. 'It sounds just a little too cosy and comfortable. No wonder he decided it wasn't what he wanted.'

'Are you insinuating that it was all my fault it went wrong?' Josie flung at him in an outraged tone. 'That he found someone else because I wasn't—wasn't *sexy* enough for him?'

'I didn't say that,' Daniel pointed out calmly.

'Oh, yes, you did. Not in so many words, but that was what you meant!'

'I just had the impression that your relationship with this ex-fiancé of yours seemed to be rather flat. No highs and lows. Friends, rather than lovers.'

'You can't possibly know that!' Josie howled at him.

'Keep your voice down,' he advised in an unruffled tone. 'Or you'll have a crowd of monks rushing in here, to see what's going on.'

'I don't care if half of Bhutan comes rushing in. I won't have you saying those kind of things to me!'

Even in the darkness, she knew that those gold-brown eyes were studying her with new interest.

'I've really struck a nerve, haven't I?' Daniel said softly. 'What's the matter, Josie? Did it worry you, as well, the fact that your fiancé didn't want to rush you into bed? That your relationship was very friendly, but that was all?'

'Of *course* we were friendly,' she retorted. 'We had a lot in common. We enjoyed the same things. And I happen to think that friendship forms a very good basis for marriage.'

'Obviously your fiancé didn't feel the same way. At least, not after he met someone who showed him what was missing from the relationship.'

For just a moment, Josie heard Derek's voice inside her head as he had tried to explain why he was leaving her for someone else. It's like a bolt of lightning, he had said. Until you experience it, you've no idea what it's like.

Josie hadn't known what he was talking about. A bolt of lightning? she had repeated to herself scornfully. What nonsense!

She still thought it was nonsense. Love was a gentle thing, based on mutual interests and a deep affection for each other. Anything as dangerous as lightning didn't come into it at all.

Daniel's gaze was still fixed on her. She didn't like that. In fact, she wished she had never got out of her sleeping-bag. She should have closed her eyes and gone straight back to sleep. Or pretended to sleep, if she couldn't manage the real thing.

'I think this conversation has got far too personal,' she said at last, in a very stiff voice.

'Do you?' Daniel kept looking at her. 'Then here's one more highly personal remark to add to all the rest. If I'd been your fiancé, I'd have wanted to rush you into bed.'

Josie started to say something, stopped, swallowed hard, and then tried again. 'I don't think it's necessary to say something like that.'

'I think that perhaps it is,' he replied softly.

'Why?' she demanded.

'I don't really know.' Even in the darkness, she could see that he was giving a faintly self-mocking smile. 'A little while ago, I thought that I had all the answers. But that was probably because I was only asking myself the easy questions.'

'I don't know what you're talking about,' Josie said flatly.

'I'm not too sure myself,' he admitted. 'I suppose this is the wrong time of night for this kind of conversation.'

'What should we be talking about, then?'

'We shouldn't be talking at all. We should be doing this.'

His kiss was soft and subtle. If Josie had expected him to kiss her—and she had to admit that the thought had crossed her mind once or twice—she hadn't expected it to be like that. All the same, she vigorously twisted her head away after only a few seconds.

'Don't!' she said crossly.

'Why? Don't you like it?'

'Liking it has got nothing to do with it,' she retorted. 'It doesn't *mean* anything. It's just—well, two mouths coming together because it feels nice.'

Daniel stared at her for a few moments in the darkness. Then he began to laugh.

'I don't think I said anything particularly funny!' Josie said, glaring at him.

'I know you don't,' he said, recovering a little, although a broad smile still covered his face. 'But I'd like to know why you think it's wrong to enjoy this "niceness" that you feel when you're kissed.'

'I didn't say that I thought it was wrong,' she snapped back with some irritation.

'Good,' said Daniel smoothly. 'Then there's no reason why we shouldn't repeat the experience, is there?'

His mouth was over hers again before she could get out any kind of protest. His kiss was a little less soft this time; more thorough and definitely more disturbing.

Josie found she was breathing rather irregularly by the time she finally managed to shake herself free.

'I don't know why you're doing this, but I wish you'd stop,' she said, her dark blue eyes flashing.

'I don't think I want to stop,' he said in an unperturbed tone. He subjected her to another kiss, and she sensed an underlying heat, a fierceness, that threatened to grow to alarming proportions. His tongue flicked round the inner warmth of her mouth in a proprietorial way, as if he had every right to subject her to this intimate probing, and his fingers inched their way lightly up and down her spine, leaving nerve-quivering shivers in their wake.

Then he stopped and let go of her. Josie's eyes, which had begun to feel oddly heavy, flew wide open again.

'Have you finally decided to behave like a gentleman?' she challenged him.

Amusement flickered across his face. 'I rarely behave like a gentleman. But, on the other hand, I don't want you to get the wrong idea about this.'

The coolness of his voice contrasted strangely with the heat that still radiated from his body. He was a man of such contradictions, thought Josie, more confused than she liked to admit by the whole episode.

'How could I get the wrong idea?' she said, somehow summoning up enough nerve to stare straight at him. 'You're making it very clear what you want from me!'

'Just as long as you realise that nothing else is on offer,' Daniel said, in that same cool tone. 'I'm not interested in relationships or any kind of commitment.'

'That's no problem, since you're the last man on earth that I'd want to have a relationship with,' retorted Josie. 'You're too cold, too cynical, too unlovable.'

For just a moment, her words seemed to strike home. His eyes narrowed and his mouth set into a taut line. He seemed about to say something, but then visibly checked himself.

'You're right,' he said at last, finally breaking the tense silence that had begun to stretch between them. 'I'm all of those things.'

Josie hadn't expected him openly to admit it. 'I expect you've got some good qualities,' she said rather grudgingly.

'I doubt it. Not any more.'

'You mean that you weren't always the way you are now? What happened to change you?'

'You ask too many questions.' His voice had become rather abrupt. 'And I've done more than enough talking for tonight.'

'You might talk a lot, but you never *tell* me anything,' Josie said frustratedly.

'And that's the way I'd prefer it to stay.'

She knew that she wasn't going to get anything more out of him tonight. And if they didn't talk, there was only one other way they could pass these last few hours of darkness. Josie hurriedly decided that option was definitely out of the question. She hadn't actually disliked his kisses, but kissing was only the first step on a long path that led to much, much more. She wasn't ready to walk along that path yet, and certainly not with Daniel Hayden.

'Well, I suppose we'd better try and get a couple more hours of sleep,' she said, edging away from him and hoping he wouldn't try to follow her. 'I expect you want to make an early start in the morning?'

'Not particularly,' he said, to her surprise. 'I want to take a look around the monastery before we leave.'

'Oh,' she said, with a touch of disappointment. For some reason, this place made her feel very edgy. She twisted her fingers together a little uneasily, and wished that they hadn't taken that wrong turning that had brought them here.

'If you want to get back into your sleeping-bag, you'll be quite safe,' Daniel told her, the dry amusement back in his voice again now. 'I promise not to lay another finger on you tonight.'

Josie quickly wriggled into the soft, quilted bag, and then stared up at him.

'Are you going to stand at that window all night?'

'I don't sleep very much,' he replied. 'I think I'll stay up for a while longer.'

She didn't like the sound of that very much. The thought of Daniel prowling silently around the room while she slept sent a fine rash of goose-pimples rushing over her skin.

On the other hand, there wasn't much she could do about it. She couldn't *force* him to sleep.

In the end, she gave a soft sigh and closed her eyes. Perhaps if she stopped looking at him, she would be able to forget he was there. And, with luck, this might be the last time they would have to share a room. They were heading for a couple of slightly larger towns, where they should be able to find an inn that could offer them separate rooms.

Josie finally fell asleep, although she then started to have slightly disturbing dreams. And Daniel Hayden didn't sleep at all for the rest of that long night.

In the morning, Josie woke up to find bright sunlight streaming through the small window. With a small groan, she sat up. She had obviously overslept.

There was no sign of Daniel. Fresh bowls of water had been provided, and so she quickly washed herself. Then she ran her fingers through her silky blonde curls to restore them to some semblance of order.

She had more or less got herself together when the door opened and Daniel walked in. Ever since she had woken up, Josie had been trying very hard not to think of what had happened last night. Now that she was face to face with Daniel, though, it was impossible not to remember those kisses he had given her. And just thinking about them made her feel strangely hot and edgy.

His gold-brown gaze slid over her. 'You look nice,' he commented.

'I look a mess,' she said rather crossly, feeling out of sorts and distinctly off balance this morning.

'Looking rather rumpled suits some women. You're one of them.'

Since Josie didn't know what to say to that, she didn't say anything at all. Instead, she busied herself rolling up her sleeping-bag and shoving the grubby, mud-stained clothes she had worn yesterday into a canvas holdall.

Daniel simply stood and watched her. For some reason, that annoyed her.

'Sometimes, I think you just brought me along with you for your entertainment,' she snapped at him. 'When you're at a loose end, you stand around and stare at me!'

'I certainly like looking at you,' he agreed in an unruffled tone.

'Why?' she demanded. 'I'm nothing special.'

He gave a leisurely shrug. 'I don't know why. I've just found that it's something I enjoy doing.'

Josie gave a rude snort. 'And when did you discover this?' she demanded.

A slow smile spread over Daniel's face. 'I think it was that last night, back in Thimphu. When I went up to the room we shared, you were asleep in bed. You looked rather gorgeous, stretched out on the sheets, and with all that bright hair spread over the pillow.'

She glared balefully at him. 'You stood there staring at me while I was in bed?'

'You were perfectly decent,' Daniel pointed out. 'In fact, you were wearing the kind of nightdress that would have been more suitable on your grandmother. And I didn't touch you.'

All the same, it made Josie feel distinctly odd inside to think of him standing there, gazing at her while she slept.

'It all sounds rather perverted to me!' she muttered darkly.

A slow smile crossed Daniel's face. 'Firstly, I don't think that a nice girl like you would recognise a perversion if it jumped up in front of you and hit you.

Secondly, I believe that simply looking at someone is generally considered to be fairly normal behaviour.'

Now he was laughing at her, and that really annoyed her. Of course, he wasn't laughing out loud—that was still a fairly rare event—but he was definitely making fun of her.

Josie slung the holdall over her shoulder and tucked the sleeping-bag under her arm. 'I'm not sure that I want to go on with this trip,' she announced bluntly. 'I think it might be a good idea if I went back to Thimphu.'

'And how do you intend to get there?' enquired Daniel calmly.

'I'll probably be able to get a lift,' she said, with much more bravado than she felt. 'Someone must be going in that direction.'

'You could wait a week, or even a month, and not find someone who was going to Thimphu. But if you're prepared to sit around here that long, I don't mind leaving you here.'

At that, Josie shivered a little. It was bad enough being in this rather spooky place with Daniel. She certainly didn't want to stay here on her own—and he knew that, damn him!

'Well, perhaps I'll go as far as the next town with you,' she muttered at last. 'Maybe I'll find someone there who'll give me a lift.'

'Now we've got that settled, are you hungry?' he asked in an unperturbed voice. 'The monks are going to give us something to eat before we leave.'

'I thought you wanted to look around the monastery?'

'I've already done that,' he told her, to her surprise. 'When?'

'While you were still asleep.'

For the first time that morning, Josie glanced at her watch. She was amazed to find that it was nearly lunchtime. She had slept even longer than she had thought.

'Why didn't you wake me up? I might have wanted to take a look around the monastery with you.'

'There are quite a few places that women aren't allowed,' Daniel told her. 'It was better that I went on my own.'

'So much for women's rights,' grumbled Josie. 'Even back home, things haven't improved that much. In places like this, they haven't even got off the ground! What would they have done if I'd just marched straight in?'

'They would probably have been deeply offended,' replied Daniel. 'And with good reason. It isn't very polite just to trample over people's religious beliefs.'

'I suppose not. I wouldn't have done it anyway,' she admitted. 'I was brought up to be very well-mannered.'

One of Daniel's eyebrows rose gently. 'I haven't noticed you being particularly polite, where I'm concerned.'

She flushed a little, mainly because he was speaking the truth. 'You just rub me up the wrong way,' she muttered.

His gold-brown eyes briefly glittered. 'I can rub you up in other ways,' he suggested softly. 'Ways that you'd like a lot better.'

'Don't start that again!' Josie warned in a sharp voice. 'I don't want anything to do with—with that kind of thing.'

'Do you mean sex?' he enquired, with a wolfish grin. 'Then why don't you just say it? It's a very simple word.'

But Josie had had quite enough of this conversation. 'I'm going to get something to eat,' she said irritably. And with that, she marched out of the room.

The monks provided them with a good, filling meal, although the main ingredient was, of course, rice. By early afternoon, they were back in the minibus and retracing the route back to the main road.

The sun was still shining brightly, although clouds were already beginning to gather around the tops of the mountains. Josie knew that it was very likely that it would begin to rain again before the afternoon was over. During the monsoon season, completely dry days were rare, although the rain often didn't arrive until quite late in the day.

Once they were back on the main road, they followed it over a great pass which led them into central Bhutan. In fact, although it was designated as a main road, it was little more than a dirt track in places, and Josie was very glad that the minibus was well sprung.

Once over the pass, the road curved in great winding loops down the side of the mountain, to the valley beyond. The light was beginning to fade again, but Josie wasn't worried. They should be in Tongsa before dark. She could already catch glimpses of it in the gathering gloom, with lights beginning to flicker in the windows of the houses, and in the huge monastery that dominated the town.

'I've never seen so many monasteries,' she said, turning to Daniel. 'Just about every town seems to have one!'

'Bhutan's a deeply religious country,' he said. Then he grinned. 'And luckily all the monasteries are very photogenic. That's very helpful, when you're planning to make a documentary.'

Josie wasn't paying much attention now, though. Instead, she was peering out of the window. 'I think it's beginning to rain again,' she said gloomily.

'It doesn't matter. We'll be in Tongsa in about fifteen minutes.'

He expertly steered the minibus around another great looping bend in the road, but it suddenly started to veer to one side, and wobbled around rather alarmingly at the same time.

'What is it?' asked Josie, sitting bolt upright.

'A puncture,' he replied briefly.

She gave a groan. 'I don't believe this! What are we going to do? Can you change a wheel? Yes, of course you can,' she said with renewed confidence. 'All men are good at things like that.'

The rain was pouring down much harder now, and Daniel looked out of the window with a darkening scowl on his face.

'And what are *you* going to do?' he asked. 'Sit here in the dry, while I get on with it?'

'There's nothing else I can do,' she said with a bright smile. 'Women are useless at anything mechanical. Everyone knows that.' In fact, she was perfectly capable of changing a flat tyre, but she certainly wasn't going to tell Daniel that. He could manage quite well on his own, she told herself with another grin.

Daniel got out of the truck, not looking at all pleased about the situation. A couple of minutes later, though, he climbed back in again, already dripping wet as the rain steadily increased in intensity.

'Don't tell me, let me guess,' said Josie, the grin rapidly fading from her face. 'There's no spare tyre.'

'Oh, there's a spare tyre, all right. But there isn't a jack.'

She pulled a face. 'Well, what do we do now? Sit here and wait for another car to come along?'

'There's not much point in that. We could stay here all night without seeing anyone at all. We'd better start walking,' Daniel decided briskly.

Josie peered out at the sheets of rain. 'Walk?' she repeated, with a total lack of enthusiasm.

'It won't take us too long to reach Tongsa. And it isn't cold out, only wet.'

'*Only* wet,' she grumbled, as she pulled on her mac, and then scrambled out of the minibus after him. Rain immediately soaked her hair and began to run down her neck. Daniel went round to the back of the bus and shovelled a few things they might need into a holdall. Then he strode on ahead, and she almost had to run to keep up with him.

The road began to turn to a muddy quagmire as water streamed across it, and Josie glared at the man in front of her. More rain, more mud, a broken-down minibus—everything this man touched seemed to turn to disaster!

Then she remembered that he had touched *her*. Goose-pimples suddenly raced over her skin, and her nerves gave a hefty twitch.

There's nothing to worry about, she assured herself. After a few more days, they would go their separate ways and probably never even see each other again.

But, as she trudged towards Tongsa, she couldn't get rid of the feeling of deep unease that had suddenly swept over her. And that feeling was definitely connected in some way that she didn't understand to Daniel Hayden.

CHAPTER SEVEN

IT WAS completely dark by the time they finally reached Tongsa. More by luck than anything else, they managed to find an inn fairly quickly. The innkeeper didn't seem in the least worried by their bedraggled appearance, and quickly ushered them inside. He didn't speak any English, and none of Daniel's half a dozen words of Bhutanese turned out to be in the least useful, but there wasn't any real communication problem.

In a remarkably short time, they had been given a room—only one room, Josie noted uneasily—water was being provided, so they could wash away the worst of the mud, and, from the innkeeper's energetic sign language, she gathered a hot meal was soon to follow.

'I bet it's rice,' she said with a grimace.

'I seem to remember your telling me that you liked rice,' Daniel reminded her.

He was pulling dry clothes out of the holdall, as he spoke. He chucked jeans, a T-shirt and a towel over to her, and then found some clothes for himself.

'When I started out on this trip, there were a lot of things I thought I liked,' Josie muttered darkly. 'But I'm rapidly going off most of them—especially rice, minibuses and *rain*.'

By the time their meal turned up, she was reasonably dry again, although still feeling edgy and bad-tempered. And she had been right. It *was* rice, spiced up with hot chillis, and accompanied by vegetables in a cheese sauce. She was so hungry, though, that she ate everything put in front of her, and enjoyed it more than she was ready to admit.

By the time they had finished eating, it was fairly late and there wasn't much they could do except go up to their room. At least they had separate beds, Josie thought with some relief. If there had only been a double bed, she would have trudged straight back to the minibus and spent the night there, rain or no rain.

She scrubbed her teeth clean, and then went over to rummage in the holdall that Daniel had brought with him. A few seconds later, she shot a black look in his direction.

'You forgot to bring my nightdress!'

'Sorry,' he said, although without any genuine trace of apology in his voice.

Josie glared at him. 'Did you do it on purpose?'

'Of course not,' he replied, beginning to sound rather irritable now. 'Anyway, it's hardly important. You can sleep in a T-shirt, can't you?'

'I suppose so,' she said grumpily. She wasn't happy about it, though. It was probably silly, but she had felt *safe* in that nightdress, with its high neck, buttoned sleeves, and the thick folds of cotton that had fallen well past her knees. Wearing just a T-shirt, most of the long line of her legs would be on show. And T-shirts were much more clinging, especially if you weren't wearing anything underneath.

Josie decided to keep on her bra and pants. At least that way she would feel respectable, even if she didn't look it!

She was well aware that she was over-reacting, but that was the way she was beginning to feel all the time when Daniel was around. He made simple things seem difficult; everyday situations somehow fraught with some unspecified danger.

Her bad temper welled up again, although she didn't know what was causing it.

'Of course, we wouldn't have got so wet and muddy if you'd checked that there was a jack in that minibus, before we set out,' she said, throwing a belligerent glance in his direction.

Daniel's own eyes began to darken noticeably. 'I don't see why that should have particularly been my job. Why didn't *you* check to see that the jack, spare tyre and tools were all there?'

'Well, I rather think that's a man's job, don't you?' she retorted.

A gleam entered his gaze. 'Then you don't believe in equality between the sexes?'

Oh, she had fallen right into that one! she told herself crossly.

'Of course I believe in equality,' she said, with a scowl. 'It's just that—well . . .' She couldn't seem to wriggle out of the corner he had backed her into, and her scowl deepened. 'I suppose that Margaret, your perfect personal assistant, checks absolutely everything before you set out on a trip.'

'Margaret's certainly very efficient,' Daniel agreed smoothly. 'And capable. She can even change a tyre, if necessary.'

'*I* can change a tyre,' Josie shot back at once. Then she immediately shut up as she remembered how she had played the helpless female, sitting in the minibus in the dry while Daniel went out in the streaming rain to deal with the puncture.

His gold-brown eyes fixed on her. 'I'll remember that, next time we get a flat tyre,' he said at last.

'If you'd really needed help, I'd have offered,' she muttered. 'But you always seem the type who can cope with everything on your own. You don't seem to need anyone else, not for anything.'

The light in his eyes slowly intensified and Josie became aware of a subtle—and rather disturbing—change in the atmosphere.

'There are some things that you definitely need someone else for,' he said, his voice sounding rather different now. 'Things that you can't do on your own—at least,' he added, a shadow of a smile touching the corners of his mouth, 'not if you want to feel any real sense of satisfaction.'

She cleared her suddenly dry throat. 'I've—I've no idea what you're waffling on about.' She forced out a huge yawn which, even to her own ears, sounded very false. 'Goodness,' she said, 'I really am tired. I think I'm going to fall asleep the moment my head hits the pillow.'

'I could easily keep you awake,' he suggested softly. 'I know a lot of ways of making someone forget how tired they are.'

'Really?' she said, somehow making her voice sound both polite and cool. 'I suppose you're talking about word games, jokes, interesting anecdotes, things like that? Well, to be honest, I'm not interested. All I want to do is sleep.'

His smile deepened. 'You're very evasive. It's like trying to pin down a butterfly.'

'Perhaps I just don't *want* to be pinned down,' she retorted, suddenly getting rather tired of this conversation.

'That's what I thought, at first,' agreed Daniel. 'But over the last couple of days I've begun to change my mind about that. I think you'd like it very much, but, because you've just had that bad experience with your ex-fiancé, you're scared of it.'

'I'm not scared of anything—or anyone,' Josie denied hotly. 'But I am going to get very fed up if we have to go through all this hassle every night. You said there wouldn't be any problems if we had to share a room, but as far as I can see, there have been nothing *but* problems. And most of them have been caused by you! You keep saying you don't want any kind of relationship with anyone, but you certainly don't act like someone who isn't interested in women!'

'I thought we'd got all this straight,' he said in a silky tone. 'I don't want a relationship, but I'm definitely interested in women.'

'You mean, you're interested in sex!' Josie threw back at him.

He shrugged. 'There's nothing wrong with that.'

'Except that I'm *not* interested.' Her dark blue eyes shone fiercely at him. 'Not interested!' she repeated vehemently.

Daniel's gold-brown gaze slid over her from head to toe, and she found it hard to suppress a deep shiver.

'I think that you are,' he said calmly. 'It's just that you haven't realised it yet. No one's taught you how to like it.'

'I had a very good relationship with my fiancé,' she insisted, her gaze still blazing. 'And I know all about sex. There's nothing you can teach me!'

In fact, that was a very long way from the truth. Her experiences with Derek had been limited to some rather fumbling and unexpectedly awkward sessions that had always stopped well short of any real intimacy. They had left her feeling curiously disappointed and wondering if there was something she hadn't done quite right, but there was no way she was ever going to admit that to Daniel Hayden!

He was standing on the far side of the room, his gold-brown gaze now resting on her with a thoughtfulness which she found disturbing. Then he began to move towards her.

'Stay away from me,' Josie said warningly.

'But I don't want to,' came his easy reply.

'I don't care what you want! When I agreed to come with you on this trip, it was on the understanding that this kind of thing wouldn't happen. You're breaking all the rules.'

'I don't remember agreeing to any particular set of rules. And even if I did, I always believe in being flexible.' Daniel's mouth curled into the kind of smile that Josie instinctively recognised as being dangerous. 'I've been trying to figure out exactly *why* I asked you to come along on this trip,' he went on. 'I know I gave you several reasons, but if you take a closer look at them none of them really stands up too well. When it comes down to it, I think I invited you on impulse. That's rather odd, because I very rarely do anything on impulse, and especially not of late. Then, when I stood in that hotel room in Thimphu, watching you sleeping, I began to understand that impulse rather better. Now and then, you meet someone who triggers off a response in you, whether you like it or not. It can be a sexual response, an antagonistic response, or even a rather odd sense of recognition, as if the stranger you've just met doesn't seem like a stranger at all. And once it happens that response doesn't just fade away, it's always there. Sometimes it even grows, and begins to get a little out of control.'

Josie stared at him. It was probably the longest speech he had ever made to her—and definitely the most disturbing!

'What exactly are you saying?' she asked warily.

He gave a faint shrug. 'I'm not sure. Except that something's happened that I never *expected* to happen.' He hesitated, then went on in a lower voice, 'When I set out on this trip, I felt dead inside. I thought I was going to go on feeling that way for a very long time, perhaps even forever. That deadness is beginning to disappear, though—and you seem to be the one who's making me feel alive again.'

'*Why* did you feel so dead?'

Evasiveness began to slide back into Daniel's eyes. 'I don't want to talk about that. Not right now.'

'You never seem to want to talk about anything,' Josie retorted. 'At least, not anything important. I don't know much more about you now than when we left Calcutta!'

'Oh, I think you know a lot more about me,' he said softly. 'And I'd like to teach you even more.'

'I've already told you that there's absolutely nothing you can teach me.' She tried to keep the alarm out of her voice as he took a few more steps forward. 'Don't come any nearer!' she yelped, as he kept up that slow advance.

'I know that you don't want me to do this, but I really think I have to,' he murmured, his eyes gleaming very brightly now.

His mouth tasted warm and fresh and male as it closed almost aggressively over hers. Josie tried to kick his shins, but he easily side-stepped her swinging foot, and then wedged her so firmly against the wall behind her that she couldn't try that manoeuvre again.

'Don't be scared,' he instructed, releasing her from the relentless pressure of his mouth for just a few moments.

'I'm *not* scared,' Josie insisted fiercely, ignoring the fact that her heart was slamming away like a giant sledge-hammer.

'Good,' said Daniel. 'Then you won't mind if we do it all over again.'

His second kiss was even more nerve-jarring than the first. Josie slowly began to realise that she really knew nothing about kissing at all. It wasn't just two mouths squashing together. With someone who really knew what he was doing—and Daniel definitely knew!—it was a whole lot more than that.

His tongue began to explore at leisure as some of the initial stiffness seeped from her limbs. Josie gulped, and then gave a small shiver as he found a particularly responsive spot.

'Nice?' he murmured.

'No,' she got out in a strangled voice, lying in her teeth.

Daniel merely grinned. She hadn't known a grin could look quite so wicked.

'If all this is coming as quite a surprise to you, then I think you should prepare yourself for some even bigger shocks,' he told her in a velvet voice.

'I'm not surprised,' she insisted, her voice annoyingly shaky. 'I've been kissed before.'

'By Derek?'

'Of course. He *was* my fiancé.'

'But not a very good lover.'

Her dark blue eyes flashed. 'How dare you say something like that?'

Daniel didn't seem perturbed. 'Why not? It's obviously the truth. He probably did you a favour when he ran off with that other girl. Let her put up with his fumblings. You deserve something better, Josie. Something more like this.'

He smoothly closed in on her before she had a chance to make any kind of indignant reply. This time, it wasn't just his mouth that provoked those small but highly disturbing pulses of pleasure. His hands slid under her T-shirt and headed unerringly for the soft swell of her breasts. He gave a small mutter of frustration when he discovered she was still wearing a bra, but dealt with it swiftly and expertly. The thin, flimsy cotton fell away, and there was nothing to protect her from his predatory fingers.

Except that they didn't *feel* predatory. They felt—very nice, Josie admitted to herself with another large gulp. And unexpectedly gentle, as if he had suddenly decided that he didn't want to alarm her by demanding too much, too soon. They didn't pinch or squeeze. Instead they slowly circled, rubbed, very lightly nipped, and then caressed in long, slow sweeps that set her heart pounding to an entirely different rhythm.

'See?' said Daniel in a voice that was a lot less relaxed than it had been just minutes ago. 'There's nothing to be alarmed about.'

But Josie thought that there was a great deal about this that was highly alarming. For a start, this had nothing to do with love. At least, not love as she had always understood it. This man *wanted* her. Just that, and no more. But the really alarming part was that he was beginning to make her want him.

It was a new experience, to feel the beginning of a hot ache inside; to want more of the touch of someone's hands and mouth. He had been right, she thought dully. She *hadn't* known anything about sex. Those awkward fumblings with Derek had just been a poor imitation of the real thing. And they had always stopped before they had gone too far.

Daniel's mouth was at work again now, moving lightly around the base of her throat, and provoking new sensations that skittered over her heated skin. He was beginning to breathe a little unsteadily, and the movements of his hands became bolder. They circled over her stomach, slid down to the waistband of the thin cotton panties she wore, and then lightly, delicately delved underneath.

'No!' she said, in a muffled voice.

His fingers immediately withdrew again. 'Not ready for that yet?' he asked, the breath rasping slightly in his throat. 'Or is it because it's all new to you?' he went on, his gold-brown eyes looking intently down into hers. 'Haven't you ever been touched like that before?'

Josie didn't want to answer his question. Anyway, what could she tell him? That, because she loved travelling so much, there hadn't been much time in her life for close personal relationships? That Derek had been the only man she had been really close to, and she was now beginning to realise that he had been almost as inexperienced as she was? She could guess how much he would laugh at her, if she ever admitted that!

'I just don't want this to go any further,' she said stiffly.

Daniel drew back from her a fraction. 'Why not?' His breathing was a little more controlled now, and a slight coolness had entered his tone.

'Because this is just—just...' Josie struggled for the right words, and finally found them. 'This is just physical contact,' she said in a clearer voice. 'There isn't any feeling behind it, anything that makes it— well, worth doing.'

It was hard to say that, when that hot ache still gripped her body, and her skin prickled and burned from his touch. Even harder when she looked into those gold tiger eyes, and caught a glimpse of something that she had never seen there before.

Then, whatever it was, it disappeared and a dark emptiness took its place. A little roughly, he pushed her away from him.

'I've never forced a woman into anything and I'm not about to start now.' He swayed towards her, as if it were an effort to stay away from her. Then he forced himself to move back again. 'Except that you're not a woman, Josie,' he said, a slightly harsh edge to his voice. 'You're still a little girl. That's why you wanted to marry a man who was a friend, not a lover. It's why you run away from any real sexual contact. You don't want to grow up. It's easier to stay your parents' pampered only child.'

Those last remarks really stung. And perhaps the reason they stung so much was that there was an element of truth in them. She *had* been a pampered child. Working in London and travelling abroad whenever she could had been an attempt to get away from the rather stifling love her parents had lavished on her, but maybe it had only been a rather half-hearted attempt. She had never been truly independent because she had never had to be. She had always known that, if anything went wrong, her parents would be there to bail her out. Because they were comfortably off, money was there if she needed it, although she would never ask for it unless it was a real emergency. And they would always take her back home without question, if she needed a bolt-hole. All she had to do was pick up a phone, and her father would immediately drive down in his large car, ready to sweep her back to warmth and comfort.

Josie didn't like the way this man was forcing her to face up to things that she usually managed to ignore. Her inexperience; the faults in her relationship with Derek; a life that had been a little too easy, so she had never really had to struggle to achieve anything.

'I've had enough of all this,' she said tightly. 'I didn't ask for any of this to happen tonight. I didn't want to be kissed or touched, and I certainly didn't want a lecture.' She grabbed hold of her jeans, which were lying near by, and began to pull them on. 'I think you're just trying to blame me for everything because I wanted to stop and you didn't.'

'No, I didn't want to stop,' Daniel agreed grimly. 'But I did,' he reminded her. 'I'll always stop at whatever point you want, which is why you don't ever have to be scared of me.'

'You don't scare me,' she said vehemently, if quite untruthfully. 'You've never scared me. Now, if you'll move out of my way, I'm getting out of here.'

'Where are you going?'

'Back to the minibus. It's probably the only place where I'll be able to get some undisturbed sleep.'

'It's pitch-dark out there,' Daniel pointed out. 'You'll get lost as soon as you leave the inn. And it's still pouring with rain.'

'I don't care,' she said fiercely. 'I'd sooner be wet and lost than stay in this room with you!'

At that, his mouth hardened. 'If I had any sense, I'd let you go. You've caused me more trouble than I ever expected—and in more ways than one. I suppose I'm responsible for you, though, which means I have to try and keep you safe until we're back in Calcutta.'

He picked up his jacket and Josie looked at him warily. 'What are you doing?'

'Since you obviously don't want to stay in the same room as me, I'm the one who had better leave.'

'Where are you going to sleep?' She hadn't meant to ask any such question. It just came out before she could stop it.

Daniel gave a twisted smile. 'Do you really care? I thought all you wanted to be sure of was that I wasn't going to sleep with *you*.'

With that, he strode out of the room. Josie sank slowly on to the nearest bed and wondered how long it was going to take her to stop shaking.

This trip was turning into a total disaster, she told herself, her entire body still gently quivering. If she had had any idea it was going to be like this, she would never have set a foot in Bhutan.

At last, the trembling eased off. She wriggled out of her jeans again, lay down on the hard bed, and found herself wondering where Daniel was right now.

She hoped it was somewhere cold, wet and uncomfortable, she muttered to herself fiercely. It was no more than he deserved, after the way he had behaved!

Then she gave a small sigh. She hadn't behaved particularly well, either. And what on earth was she going to say to him, when she saw him again in the morning? How was she even going to be able to look into those gold-brown eyes?

With those questions still whirling round inside her confused head, and her body feeling tense and unsettled, she pulled the cover right over her and made the first of many totally unsuccessful attempts to go to sleep.

Josie woke from a light, dream-racked doze, unglued her heavy eyes, and then gave a groan as all the events of last night came tumbling back into her mind.

Bright light was filtering in through the window, which meant that it was time to get up. She didn't want to face the day, though—or Daniel. She would have liked to have stayed hidden under the covers until darkness fell again.

She had the feeling that if she stayed in bed too long, however, Daniel would simply come in and haul her out. He probably wasn't the least embarrassed about what had happened last night. Just disappointed that he hadn't been able to get any further!

And was she embarrassed? she asked herself. No, she finally decided, that was entirely the wrong way to describe the way she felt. In fact, she didn't think that there *was* a word to describe the way she had felt last night. And there were still some very odd emotions churning round inside her this morning.

Wearily, she crawled out of bed. After a quick wash and a half-hearted effort to restore some kind of order to her tangled hair, she opened the door of their room and peered out.

There was no sign of Daniel. A faint sensation of panic began to gather inside her. What if he had gone off and left her here? Decided that he had had enough, and just abandoned her?

Josie swallowed hard. The people of Bhutan were friendly and hospitable, and the country itself was beautiful, even when it was raining. She definitely didn't want to be stranded here on her own, though. She was beginning to discover that she wasn't quite as independent as she had liked to think.

Just then, she heard the sound of Daniel's voice. Her stomach immediately flipped in a very uncomfortable way, and a gentle shiver ran right up the length of her spine.

A couple of minutes later, he came up to their room.

'Good, you're up,' he said shortly. 'Are you ready to leave?'

'Have you fixed the minibus?' she asked in surprise.

'I found someone who could lend me a jack, and I've changed the wheel.'

'You must have been up for ages!'

'Since dawn,' Daniel replied briefly. 'I told you, I never sleep much.'

And especially after last night, Josie thought with a sinking feeling. She took another quick, nervous look at his closed face, and then silently sighed. This was all going to be very difficult. Then irritation gradually began to stir inside of her. All of this was *his* fault, she told herself. *He* was the one who had created these problems. Everything had been going really well until he had suddenly decided to turn a fairly friendly relationship into something a lot more complicated and difficult to handle.

She began to glare at him, and he immediately glared straight back. He seemed as on edge as she was.

'Are we leaving right away?' Josie asked at last in a very stiff voice.

'Unless you can think of one good reason why we should stay here any longer,' came his rather brusque reply.

She thought of mentioning the fact that she hadn't even had breakfast yet, but, after another look at his darkened eyes, rather hurriedly decided against it. Anyway, she wasn't in the least hungry. Spending time with Daniel Hayden was as good as being on a crash diet. He could put you right off food!

Josie followed him out of the inn, into a morning that was brilliantly sunny. Everything was very fresh and green after the torrential rain of last night, the air tasted sweet, and in any other circumstances she would probably have thought it a glorious day.

The minibus was parked outside the inn, and she climbed inside. Daniel got in beside her and started up the engine. Then, without saying another word, he drove out of Tongsa at an unnecessarily fast speed.

Josie had thought that, after last night, he might decide to head straight back to Thimphu. He sent the minibus roaring off in the opposite direction, though, deeper into the countryside.

It was impossible to keep up that high speed for long. The road soon began to deteriorate, and become pitted with muddy ruts. He still drove far too fast for the conditions, and Josie bounced and rattled around inside the minibus until her bones ached. In the end, her temper finally snapped.

'If you're going to drive like a maniac all day, I'd sooner get out and walk!'

Daniel reduced speed just a fraction. 'Sorry,' he said tersely.

'No, you're not!' Her dark blue eyes blazed fiercely at him. 'What is this? Some sort of punishment for last night, because I wouldn't—wouldn't...' She couldn't quite finish. The words stuck in her throat.

'Wouldn't go to bed with me?' His own voice was drier now, and less taut. 'I don't think someone should be punished for not wanting me. This is just my way of working off the last of a lot of frustration.'

'Well, I wish you'd driven around on your own for a couple of hours, and got it out of your system before we set off!' Josie said crossly. 'Apart from anything else, it would have given me time to have had some breakfast. Although I'm rather glad now that I didn't. I've never been travel-sick in my life, but if I rattle around in this minibus much longer, that could all change!'

To her relief, Daniel reduced speed even further. He seemed a little more relaxed than when they had first set out, and some of the darkness had lifted from his face.

Josie began to breathe rather more easily. Daniel Hayden was difficult enough to cope with at the best of times. She wasn't sure that she could deal with him at all if he sank into a prolonged black mood.

The countryside all around them was beginning to look more isolated. They only occasionally caught glimpses of houses tucked into the hillsides, and the road was beginning to wind through great stretches of woodland. The branches often closed right overhead, with thin shafts of sunlight breaking through to dapple the ground underneath with golden circles of light.

After they had gone a couple more miles, Daniel turned his head and glanced at her. 'Do you want to talk about last night?' he asked, to her surprise.

'Talk about it?' she echoed warily. 'No, I don't think so. What is there to say?'

He gave a small shrug. 'I'm not sure. But sometimes it's better to discuss these things, rather than to push them away and just pretend they haven't happened.'

But Josie didn't think she wanted to get involved in that kind of conversation.

'I'm not sure—I don't usually——'

'You don't usually talk about sex?' he asked, the very faintest note of amusement beginning to creep back into his voice.

Josie frowned. He was trying to make her sound immature again! It really irritated her when he did that.

'I don't think that talking about it would achieve anything useful,' she said at last, in what she hoped was a very firm voice. 'Anyway, I don't know why you're suddenly so keen on discussing things. *You're* the one who usually doesn't want to talk about anything in the least personal.'

'Perhaps I'm beginning to change my mind about that,' he said, his tone even more relaxed now. 'You said last night that you didn't know anything about me. Well, I'm willing to answer a few questions this morning. What do you want to know?'

Josie was so astonished that she couldn't think of a single thing to ask him. The minibus rattled along for several minutes before a question finally popped into her head.

'What about your family?' she said. 'You told me that they all liked travelling, but nothing more. Start by telling me about them.'

'My father works for a large oil company,' Daniel said comfortably. 'He's a trouble-shooter. Since the company operates virtually world-wide, he can be sent almost anywhere, and at very short notice. Whenever she can, my mother goes with him. She loves travelling as much as he does. Neither of them spend very much time at home. My two brothers are both younger than I am. And, before you ask, I'm thirty-four,' he added. 'One of my brothers works in America, in the music business, and the other, the youngest, left university only last year. He's travelling around Europe at the moment, seeing something of the world before he decides what kind of job to go after. He's trained as an engineer, so there'll be plenty of job opportunities that'll be open to him when he does finally decide to settle down. That won't be for a while yet, though. He's planning to go to South America and Australia, after he's seen all of Europe.'

'Since you're all coming and going so much, I should think you hardly ever see each other,' commented Josie.

'We bump into each other more often than you'd expect. Although I often meet up with members of my family in some rather odd places.'

'Like having dinner with your aunt Katherine in a Maharaja's house in the middle of Calcutta?' enquired Josie.

He grinned. 'I like Aunt Katherine. She's very straightforward, intelligent and adventurous. And although she's pretty down to earth, she's got a lot of interesting—and unusual—friends.'

'I'm beginning to think your entire family is unusual!'

'Including me?' he asked, one eyebrow gently lifting.

'I'm not sure yet. I'll tell you when I know more about you.'

'What else do you want to know?'

'Just about everything. You've still told me next to nothing about yourself, only about your family,' Josie complained. 'You're probably the most secretive man I've ever known!'

'Since you can probably count the men you've known on one hand—and still have fingers to spare—I should think it's rather hard to make comparisons.'

'Why do you keep doing that?' she said with a quick rush of annoyance.

'Doing what?'

'Making me sound like some inexperienced little idiot, who'd have trouble recognising a man even if she came face to face with one! I'm twenty-three—nearly twenty-four,' Josie told him hotly. 'I've been engaged, and I had a very healthy relationship with my fiancé.'

'It can't have been *that* healthy,' Daniel pointed out with infuriating calmness, 'or he wouldn't have gone off with someone else.'

'There you go again!' she yelled at him, suddenly losing her temper completely. 'Making out that it was all *my* fault that he went off. Are you getting back at me because of last night? Because I wouldn't sleep with you? Are you saying that if I'd slept with Derek he'd have stayed with me? That I should have used sex to keep him? That that's all a man really wants from a woman?'

She was bright red and boiling angry by now. It was impossible to have a normal conversation with this man! He always twisted things around; kept all his own secrets and yet probed deeper and deeper into hers.

Daniel shot a level glance at her, his gold-brown eyes revealing absolutely nothing at all.

'Those are all your words, not mine,' he said evenly. 'Perhaps it's what you think, Josie. Or maybe when you were with Derek you were made to feel sexually inadequate. You didn't really *want* to sleep with him because you didn't like feeling like that. And now you're afraid to try again, in case you feel that way with all men.'

That was so close to the truth that Josie didn't even answer. She was suddenly very frightened of what she might say. This man seemed to be able to get right under her skin and dig out all her most private secrets and fears.

She turned her head and stared out of the window, refusing even to look at him. The long silence stretched on and on, until her nerves felt almost ready to fracture from the strain. And she wished, more than anything, that they were back home, driving along a crowded road in England. Then she could just jump out and hitch a lift, catch a bus or a train, flag down a taxi, *anything* that would get her a long, long distance away from Daniel Hayden.

CHAPTER EIGHT

HALFWAY through the afternoon, they left the great stretches of woodland behind them, and the road once again became a heart-stopping curve around the mountainside. Soon they were dropping down into a sunlit valley, with a village gathered at the foot of an outcrop of rock. On top of the rock was a white-walled castle that seemed to dominate the whole valley, which basked tranquilly in the sunshine.

Daniel drove past the castle and a little further along the valley. Then he turned off on to a small side-road, which led them to a group of wooden cabins which stood at the gates of a rather run-down palace.

'This all belongs to the princess,' he said briefly. 'She's given us permission to stay here tonight. In the morning, we'll head back to Thimphu. I've think I've seen everything I need to see.'

Josie let out a silent sigh of relief. The end of this interminable journey was finally in sight!

They unloaded from the minibus everything they would need for the night. There was only one cabin suitable for sleeping in. The others contained some rather ancient stores of food, while a couple had large holes in the roof. If the rain started up again—and the clouds were already gathering rather ominously, blotting out the bright sunshine—then anyone sleeping there would quickly be soaked.

'I'll spend the night in the minibus,' Daniel said rather tersely. He threw his sleeping-bag back in, and then walked off, as if he needed to get away from her for a while.

Josie let out a pent-up breath as he disappeared from sight. She seemed to be tense all the time now, when he was around.

On rather shaky legs, she walked into the cabin where she was to spend the night. It had a bathroom of sorts, with a lot of ancient and elaborate plumbing, but none of it seemed to work very well. With regret, she abandoned her plans for a long soak in a hot bath, to try and get rid of some of the tension which riddled her body. Instead, she washed in cold water, which only added to the goose-pimples which skittered at regular intervals over her skin.

When she had finally finished, she decided that she ought to try and find something to eat. Her last meal had been nearly twenty-four hours ago, and, although she still seemed to have no appetite, she knew that deliberately starving herself wouldn't make her feel any better.

Daniel returned just as she was sorting through the provisions stacked in one of the other cabins. As soon as he walked through the doorway, she began to gabble nervously.

'There's a lot of food here, but I don't know if there's anything we can actually use. There's rice, of course—sacks of it! And chillis. And some kind of dried meat, hanging on string. Heaven knows what that is!'

Daniel went over to look at it. 'Yak meat,' he told her.

'Well, I'm sure it's very nice, if you like that kind of thing,' Josie said rather faintly. There were a pile of tins in one corner. She picked one up and looked at the label. 'Pilchards,' she said. 'Can you eat pilchards with rice?'

'You probably could, if you had to. Luckily, we don't,' Daniel said. 'The innkeeper back in Tongsa provided us with enough food to see us through until tomorrow. It's in the minibus.'

'Why didn't you tell me?' she grumbled, as she followed him out of the cabin.

'Because I wasn't sure if you were talking to me,' he replied, a faint light gleaming in the depths of his eyes now.

When they reached the minibus, Daniel pulled out a box. 'Eggs, chicken, bread, fresh fruit—there should be enough here for a couple of decent meals,' he pronounced, as he rummaged through the different packages. 'With luck, we shouldn't have to resort to the pilchards or yak meat.'

'Thank heavens for that!' Josie said fervently. 'Where are we going to eat? Inside the cabin?'

'Unless you want me to have my meals inside the minibus, as well as sleeping in it.'

'Of course I don't,' she said rather crossly. 'You know that.'

'As far as you're concerned, I know hardly anything at all,' Daniel replied, rather disconcertingly. 'And you make things even more complicated by changing your mind—and your mood—every five minutes.'

'I do not!' she denied indignantly. '*You're* the one who has all the difficult moods.'

'Me?' he repeated, in what seemed like genuine surprise. 'I've always thought that I'm very easy to get along with.'

'Easy!' said Josie, with a snort. 'Who on earth told you that?'

He shrugged. 'Well, perhaps I've been behaving rather out of character lately. In fact, we both seem to have been rather on edge.'

'That's not very surprising,' she retorted. 'Hardly a single thing on this trip has turned out the way I expected!'

'Nor the way that I expected it,' he said drily. 'It certainly hasn't been the kind of trip I usually make, when I'm making preliminary preparations for a documentary. I haven't done half the things I intended to do, spoken to as many local people as I'd have liked, or explored as much of the countryside as I should have.'

'And that's my fault?' Josie said indignantly.

'You've certainly been rather—distracting.'

'You didn't have to let yourself *be* distracted,' she pointed out.

'When we started out, I didn't think that I *could* be distracted,' Daniel said in the same dry tone.

Josie was silent for a while after that. Eventually she said, a little hesitantly, 'Are you going back to Thimphu tomorrow because of me? Because you don't want to travel around with me any more?'

He shook his head. 'I'm going back because I don't seem to be getting anywhere with this project. I've cut through some of the red tape involved if I want to go ahead with the documentary, and I've travelled around enough to make sure that the film crew won't have any major problems with the roads and accommodation. Once I'm back in England, though, I'm going to hand the project over to someone else.'

'Why?'

Daniel was silent for quite a long time before finally answering. 'Because I don't seem to be able to look at Bhutan through the eyes of a documentary maker. To me, it's always going to be the place where I've found a certain kind of—peace.'

'Peace?' echoed Josie, startled. 'The last couple of days seem to have been anything except peaceful!'

He shrugged. 'Everyone sees things in different ways. I can only tell you how this trip has seemed to me. Although I suppose it might be because these last few days have been so very different from all the days that went before.'

'And what were they like?' Josie asked curiously.

His face went oddly blank. 'Hell on earth,' he said flatly.

And she had enough sense not to ask any more questions, not right now, with the air between them shimmering with a sudden, dangerous tension.

A large spot of rain splashed on her face, followed by a couple of others.

'We'd better get into the cabin,' she said, in a subdued tone. 'It's going to pour in a few minutes. And it's beginning to get dark.'

For a few moments, she thought that Daniel was going to stay out there, in the rain and the gathering gloom. Then he picked up the box of food and followed her inside.

Josie lit a small lamp, which gave off a soft glow. Then she unpacked the food. They ate in silence, but she didn't feel uncomfortable about the lack of conversation. The tension which had sprung up between them earlier seemed to have drifted away again, and it felt cosy and warm inside the cabin.

When they had finished eating, she carefully re-packed the food that was left. They could have it in the morning, for breakfast. It would certainly be better than pilchards!

It was completely dark outside now. Daniel still hadn't said a word since entering the cabin, although he was on his feet now, pacing a little restlessly over to the window and looking out rather broodingly at the rain-soaked night outside.

'Er—perhaps we'd better try and get some sleep, if you want to make an early start in the morning,' Josie suggested rather tentatively.

He turned round to face her, and his gold-brown eyes positively glowed in the soft light streaming from the lamp.

'I never said that I wanted to make an early start.'

'I just—well—assumed that you wanted to get back to Thimphu as quickly as possible,' she said, her voice tripping over the words a little, for some reason.

'Why would I want to rush back to Thimphu? Or Calcutta? Or England?' he said softly. 'There's nothing—no one—waiting for me in any of those places.'

'I thought that was the way you liked it. The cat who walks by himself—that's you, isn't it?' Except that she had always thought of him as a tiger, not a cat. With the dangerous gold eyes of a hunting animal.

Daniel began to advance slowly. It briefly crossed Josie's mind that this would be a very good time to back away. Then it was hard to think of anything at all, at least not while she was pinned down by that gold-brown gaze.

'That *was* me,' he agreed softly. 'But I've discovered that I'm getting very tired of being on my own.'

She swallowed hard. 'Well, once you're back home you can change your life, if you want to. You must have friends. For all I know, you might even have a wife.'

'I don't have a wife,' he told her. A slightly grim note entered his voice. 'I very nearly did, at one point. But, like you, I had a lucky escape.'

Josie's own eyes momentarily flared. 'I didn't feel very lucky when I lost Derek!'

'Maybe not. But he was wrong for you, Josie. Surely you've realised that by now?'

'How can you know he was wrong for me? You've never even met him!'

'I didn't have to meet him,' Daniel answered evenly. 'I only had to feel the way you tensed up when I first touched you. No one who's had a good relationship reacts like that.'

'I should think almost *everyone* reacts like that when they're jumped on by someone they hardly even know!' she retorted.

His mouth curled up at the corners into a smile that made her nerve-ends jangle almost painfully.

'You know me,' he said.

'I certainly don't,' Josie insisted. 'How can I, when you'll never talk about yourself?'

'You might not know too much about me. Not yet. But you do know me.'

While they had been talking, he had stood still. As silence fell between them again, he began to walk forwards, moving slowly but with an air of intent that definitely alarmed Josie.

'What—what do you want me to do, now this trip's nearly over?' she gabbled, determined to get the conversation going again if that was what it took to keep him a safe distance away from her.

'Do?' Daniel repeated, sounding faintly surprised.

'Well, you brought me along because you wanted someone who'd look at Bhutan from a woman's point of view, didn't you?' She was still gabbling, but couldn't seem to stop. 'So, what should I do now? Make notes? Give you some kind of written report?'

'I think you should stop talking,' Daniel told her in a voice that was quite calm, and yet still sent a nervous *frisson* right through her, from head to toe.

But that was the one thing that Josie didn't want to do. 'I like talking,' she blabbered on. 'In fact, perhaps I could *tell* you what I think of Bhutan.' She was turning into a modern-day Scheherazade, she thought, suppressing a slightly hysterical giggle. Chattering non-stop to try and keep Daniel Hayden at bay! Well, she might not be able to manage a thousand and one nights, but surely she could keep it up for a couple of hours? By then, with luck, he would be so tired—and so bored!—that he would simply fall asleep.

'Where would you like me to start?' she prattled on. 'From the point when we first landed in Bhutan?'

'Shut up, Josie,' said Daniel, in the kind of tone that it was very hard to disobey.

All the same, she managed to squeeze out one word. 'Why?' she asked in a rather squeaky voice.

'Because when you're talking non-stop, it's almost impossible to do this.'

'This' turned out to be the kiss that she had been expecting—and half dreading—ever since he had begun to move towards her. It was an odd sort of kiss, though. A little rough, yet slightly tentative; shorter than she had expected, and not followed immediately by another. It was almost as if he wanted to gauge her reaction before going any further.

Well, this was the time to let him know exactly what she thought about this situation, Josie told herself firmly. Pull back, give him a black look, and then tell him that you certainly don't want to go through all this again.

Except that part of her *did* want to go through it. That realisation came as a distinct—and very unwelcome—shock. It also left her shaken and vulnerable—not a good state to be in when Daniel Hayden was so very close!

With a huge effort, Josie pulled herself together. She was at a low ebb right now, she excused herself. Her broken engagement; the sudden decision to go ahead with the trip to Bhutan; all the long hours of travelling—she was bound to be feeling out of sorts and behaving rather oddly. It was like an attack of emotional jet lag. She needed a lot of rest and quiet in soothing surroundings, so that she could slowly get back to normal again. Coming to Bhutan after her broken engagement had been just about the worst thing she could have done. She could see that very clearly now. She should have stayed at home and licked her wounds in private, until she was ready to face the world again. Instead, she was in a strange country, trying to avoid the predatory arms of a man who suddenly seemed determined to fan a small spark of interest into a great roaring blaze.

All the time these thoughts were running through her head, Daniel was simply standing there, watching her. He hadn't touched her again, or made another attempt to kiss her. He seemed to be waiting for her to decide what she wanted to do next.

'I—er——' Her voice cracked, and she cleared her throat rather noisily before trying again. 'I don't think it's a good idea for us to get involved. Not in any way at all.'

'What kind of involvement did you think I had in mind?' Daniel asked silkily.

'You know very well!' she said with a sudden spurt of annoyance. Then she got hold of herself again. She wasn't going to allow him to provoke her. She wanted to sound calm, uninterested, detached. 'It wouldn't work. We don't—fit together.'

'You mean that we're not good friends? And that's your idea of the ideal partner? But I'm not looking for a friend,' he told her softly.

Josie had a very good idea what he *was* looking for, and she took a rather hurried step backwards. 'I just think that it would be best if we simply left things as they are.'

Daniel moved forward, so that the gap between them closed again. 'And I think that we both need something from each other.'

'No,' she said, but without as much conviction as she had intended.

He ignored her reply, and his voice began to take on a husky undertone. 'Right now, for different reasons, I think that we need to be together.'

We certainly don't, she meant to say. Meant to say it, but the words just didn't come out. She didn't know why. They stuck somewhere in her dry throat, and, by the time she had finally managed to work them loose, it was too late. Daniel had already moved forwards for the last time, as if something she had said or done—or *hadn't* said or done—had finally made up his mind for him.

His kiss this time was entirely different from the one he had given her before. In fact, from any he had ever given her. Hard and probing, as if he wanted to push her to the limits, and beyond, exploring just how much pleasure could be wrenched from the simple contact of two mouths.

Josie just had time for a couple of dazed thoughts—that she had never been kissed like this in her life before, that she hadn't known it was possible to *be* kissed like this. Then the first kiss was followed by a second that literally took her breath away. At the same time his hands moved into action, forcefully extending the areas of pleasure until they seemed to spread right over her body, even sinking deep below her skin and setting off a dull, sweet ache somewhere inside her.

He burrowed under her T-shirt and gave a grunt of satisfaction as he found the softness of her breasts. Josie's skin erupted in waves of heat and she found it hard to believe that one man's touch could produce nothing more than a slight feeling of embarrassment, while another's could make her flesh seem to melt.

'Sometimes, it just seems like the right time and the right place and the right person,' Daniel murmured thickly, lifting his mouth from hers for a few moments. 'And when it's like that, it's very, *very* good.'

Josie tried to say something, but still couldn't. She seemed to have run out of words. Anyway, what would she have said if it were possible? That she wanted him to stop? But she didn't! Her senses were full of the sight, sound and smell of him, and it was like an instantly addictive drug; she wanted more and more.

And he was more than willing to give it. He turned his attention to her breasts again, and then growled when he couldn't find easy access. Her T-shirt was swiftly pulled over her head, and her bra unfastened and discarded, thrown impatiently to one side. Then, with her naked upper body open and vulnerable to him, he proceeded to caress it with such startling gentleness that any fear of him that might have been lurking deep inside Josie simply ebbed away on a long, slow flow of pleasure.

After a while, he tossed one of the sleeping-bags on to the floor and made her lie down. As if sleepwalking, she obeyed. She had the unnerving feeling that he could make her do absolutely anything tonight.

His tongue licked delicately round the small pink tips of her breasts again, and the breath seemed to lock in her throat. At the same time, his fingers moved down to her waist, deftly unzipped her jeans and then drifted underneath the coarse denim.

Josie closed her eyes and shuddered. He had been right, she thought numbly. She hadn't known anything at all about what happened between a man and a woman.

'This is all becoming a little one-sided,' Daniel murmured in her ear. 'I like to be touched, as well as to touch.'

She wasn't sure where to start. Rather tentatively, she undid the buttons on his shirt. The skin of his chest felt nice, warm and supple, and so she became a little bolder, exploring further. He shrugged off his shirt so that she had free access to the broad line of his back, the powerful set of his shoulders and the curve of his spine. He was breathing rather heavily now, but managing to stay in control. Inexperienced though she was, Josie instinctively sensed that and felt safe.

The lamp they had lit earlier was still throwing out its soft light, and so she could see his face as he loomed over her again, his touch not quite so gentle now. The gold-brown eyes gleamed very brightly and heightened colour showed along the ridge of his cheekbones.

Josie stared up at him and was amazed at how familiar he seemed. He had been right, she thought giddily. She *did* know him.

He shifted restlessly and began to pull off her jeans, impatient now to see all of the long, graceful lines of her body. She saw his tanned hands move over her own paler skin, and felt the heat rise inside her as he caressed it. She raised her own palms and placed them against his chest. Then she let her hands move slowly down, tracing the strong outline of his body, until she felt his inner muscles clench and jump in involuntary response.

His breathing quickened still further and he shrugged off the last of his own clothes. Hot and aroused, he pressed himself against her as if seeking some temporary relief. It only triggered off more urgent bursts of pleasure, though, and Josie found herself moving a little frantically against him, wanting to get closer, even closer, so that there wasn't even a hair's breadth of space between them.

In a hoarse voice, Daniel said her name. Then said it again. She opened her heavy eyes wider, saw his face so near that it was almost a blur, and very slowly shook her head. Hard to believe that this was happening. Even harder to believe that she wanted it to happen.

His mouth closed over hers in a kiss that was an odd mixture of gentleness and aching desire. Then he lifted his head again, his own eyes as dark and heavy as hers.

'I told you once that I'd always stop whenever you wanted,' he said huskily. 'Another couple of minutes, though, and I won't be able to keep that promise. So if you want to stop, it had better be right now.'

She looked up into those gold-brown eyes, felt for a few moments as if she were sinking right into them, and then something very odd seemed to happen to her. Her skin felt as if it had suddenly caught fire, her heart stopped beating and then started up again with a painfully hard thud, and every nerve in her body ran riot for a few brief seconds, as if they had been lanced and had responded with a jagged, yet sweet pain.

Josie's eyes flew wide open with shock. What was happening to her? Then she instinctively *knew*.

It was the bolt of lightning! Derek had warned that it might hit her one day, and now it had. She finally knew what it felt like; knew that you were never the same once it had hit you.

She had thought she was making love and instead she had suddenly fallen *in* love. Or perhaps it wasn't so sudden. Maybe it had been creeping up on her for some time, waiting to catch her at her most vulnerable moment.

'Josie?' said Daniel. His voice was still husky, but he sounded a little more in control now. 'What is it?'

She shook her head. She couldn't seem to say anything.

His hand ran lightly over the length of her and she quivered violently under his touch. His breathing began to quicken again and the pressing insistent hardness of his body burned against her. Josie was aware of every hot, velvet inch of him in a way that she had never been aware of anyone in her life before.

He seemed to realise that something wasn't quite right, though. His hand stopped its devastating exploration of the soft, aching curves of her body, and he looked down at her.

'What is it?' he said again.

'A bolt of lightning,' she muttered rather incoherently.

'Lightning?' He shook his head. 'There isn't any lightning. It's still raining, but there isn't a storm.'

'Yes, there is. But it's here, inside.' Josie knew that she wasn't making any sense, but she couldn't help it.

Daniel moved restlessly, as if the very last thing he wanted to do right now was to talk. At the same time, though, he made a clear effort to keep the very obvious desires of his body under some kind of control. He took a couple of deep, rather ragged breaths and then let his gold-brown gaze rest on her own troubled dark blue eyes.

'If you don't want to do this, or if you're scared, or nervous, or there's something else that's making you look at me the way you are right now, then *tell* me. We can work it out, I can put it right.'

'No, you can't,' she whispered shakily. 'It's too *late* to put it right.'

His gaze hardened a fraction. 'If you feel like that, why the hell did you let me get this far? Why didn't you stop me earlier, before I——?' He broke off, gave a frustrated growl, and rolled away from her, still aroused and breathing unevenly.

'You don't understand,' Josie almost cried. 'I'm not saying that I don't want you. I do! But I've done something very stupid. And I don't think you're going to like it,' she finished in a much smaller voice.

Daniel sat up, his eyes very bright. 'What have you done, Josie?' he asked softly. 'I think you'd better tell me.'

She chewed her lip in an agony of nervousness and confusion. 'I *did* tell you,' she muttered at last. 'It's the bolt of lightning. Derek told me that it would hit me one day, but I just didn't believe him.'

'I don't think this is a very good time to bring up the subject of Derek,' he said a little grimly.

'It's all right to talk about him, because he doesn't matter,' Josie said in a slightly clearer voice. 'I didn't love him, I can see that now. At least, I did love him, but only as a close friend. Not in the important way, the way that really counts. The way that I'm starting to feel about you,' she finally blurted out, wanting to get the words out before she became too scared to death to say them.

Daniel looked at her for a long, long time, and the expression in his eyes completely chilled her. Then, without saying a word, he got up, pulled on his clothes and began to walk towards the door.

'Where are you going?' Josie asked, hardly able to believe that he was just going to walk out on her.

'Out,' he said briefly.

'But it's dark and it's raining!'

'That doesn't matter.'

'You just want to get away from me, don't you?' she said, her tone suddenly becoming flat. 'I shouldn't have said anything about love, should I? You don't want to hear it.'

His face was shadowed now, and impossible to read. 'I just don't think I can handle it right now,' he said after a long, tense pause.

'Then when *do* you think you'll be able to handle it? Tomorrow? Next week? Not for a couple of months?' Josie couldn't seem to control her sudden spurt of anger at the lousy trick her emotions had played on her, making her fall for the wrong man. Wasn't anything in her life going to go right?

'I don't think this is a good time to talk about this,' Daniel said tightly. 'Perhaps in the morning, when we're both feeling less——'

'Less what?' Josie demanded. She had pulled her own T-shirt back on now, and felt a little less vulnerable than when she had been naked. 'Less emotional? But you don't *have* any emotions. At least, none that you're prepared to show. That's your problem, Daniel.'

'Don't you think I know that?' There was a slightly bitter note in his voice now. 'Credit me with enough intelligence to recognise my own failings.'

'But *why* are you like that?'

For quite some time she thought he wasn't going to answer. He stood by the doorway, obviously still wanting to leave. Then he took a couple of slow, reluctant steps back into the room.

'Why am I like this?' he said softly. 'Because it's safer. Because some women are so good at inflicting pain, and I don't want to go through that kind of experience ever again.'

Josie swallowed rather hard. 'You had a bad relationship?' It was funny how much it suddenly hurt to think of Daniel being involved with someone else.

'Yes, I had a bad relationship,' he agreed, after another long pause.

'These things sometimes happen,' she said in a subdued voice. 'Most people eventually pick themselves up and try again.'

'And what the hell would you know about it?' Daniel asked with sudden harsh vehemence. 'You, with your big, innocent eyes, your almost untouched body and your childish ideas about love?' He ignored the shock that clearly showed on her face, and went on in the same grating tone. 'You've no idea what two people can do to each other when a relationship starts to go wrong. The subtle twists of the knife because you know each other's vulnerable spots, the extra special ways you find to cause pain and permanent damage.'

Josie was shaking a little now, but she wanted—needed—to know more. 'If things were that bad, why didn't you just walk away from each other?' she asked unsteadily.

His gold-brown eyes flared. 'Because sometimes the sex is still so good that you don't want to leave. You can't understand that, can you?' he challenged her. 'Or perhaps you're just beginning to understand, after tonight,' he added, making the colour rise hotly in her face. 'But even if you do understand, you probably don't approve.'

'I think that what people do with their lives is their own business,' she said, managing to keep her voice more even this time. 'Tell me more about—this woman.'

It was such a long time before he said anything that she thought he was going to keep it locked inside himself. Eventually, though, he began to speak.

'I met her at a party. After five minutes, we knew that we wanted each other. Two hours later, we were in bed together, and that set the pattern for our relationship. She was an actress. She was good, but she couldn't get any decent parts, and that twisted something inside her. She saw other actresses getting parts that she would almost literally have killed for, and that gnawed away at her. She was never very easy to live with, and it got worse as time went by. She began to change into someone I hardly recognised.'

'Did you love her?' asked Josie in a slightly choked voice. 'In the beginning, I mean, before she changed?'

'I don't know. Ours was always a very physical relationship, it was what held us together. Some people say that's just another side of love, and, if they're right about that, then I suppose I loved her.'

Josie wished she hadn't asked that question. In fact, she wished she had never started this conversation at all. A perverse curiosity made her push it even further, though.

'What happened? What made you finally break up?'

His face became more grim. 'Are you sure you want to know?'

'Yes,' she said with some determination.

'She went for an audition for a part in a film, not the leading role but a good supporting role that would get her noticed. She got the part, but at the same time she became pregnant.'

'Oh,' said Josie, in a soft whisper.

'We'd been careful, but sometimes being careful just isn't enough.' Daniel's face changed, and his mouth drew into a tight line. 'She didn't tell me she was pregnant. In fact, she made very sure that I didn't know about it. A couple of weeks later, she said she was going up north for a day or two, to stay with an old friend. There wasn't any friend, of course. She spent those couple of days having an abortion.'

Josie's throat seemed to close up and she couldn't say anything.

'When she came back, she calmly sat down and told me what she'd had done,' Daniel went on in a fractured voice. 'Described it in some detail. Enjoyed telling me how she'd had my child sucked out of her. It seemed to give her some perverse kind of pleasure. She liked my helplessness, my anger. She sat there smiling at me, as if she'd done something very clever.'

'How could she do something like that?' Josie said with a small but violent shiver.

'Part of me could understand why she had wanted the abortion,' said Daniel, his eyes curiously dead now. 'She had finally got the big break she'd been waiting for, for such a long time. It must have seemed like a particularly cruel twist of fate when she found she was pregnant. It wasn't a good time for her to have a baby. It was the way she got rid of it, though, that really destroyed me. The way that she wanted me to *know* what she'd done. She couldn't wait to tell me all the stomach-churning details. She didn't give a damn about the child she'd destroyed. She just loved the feeling of power that it gave her over me. The fact that there was absolutely nothing I could do about it—except perhaps try to kill her, through sheer rage,' he finished grimly.

'And did you?' asked Josie in a low, trembling voice. 'Try to kill her?'

'I wanted to, but I didn't touch her. Perhaps it was because I knew that she would almost have enjoyed it. She liked a little violence—it really aroused her. There was a sick streak in her that I hardly noticed when I first met her, but which seemed to come nearer and nearer to the surface during the couple of years that we were together.'

She looked at him through eyes that were rather blurred. 'Do you blame yourself for that? Do you think that *you* brought out that sick streak in her?'

'I don't know. I don't think so, but I can't be certain.'

'You're not a violent man.' Josie said that with complete certainty, although she had no idea how she could be so sure of that fact.

Daniel smiled thinly. 'There were times when she pushed me very close to it. I don't want to risk that ever happening again.'

'You were gentle enough with me.'

'One night doesn't cure everything that's gone wrong in the past. I don't trust myself. And I don't trust relationships.'

'Perhaps I can help you to get some of that trust back again,' Josie said steadily.

His gold-brown gaze fixed on her, and for a moment a flicker of hope seemed to lighten his eyes. Then it died away again.

'I don't think anyone can do that, not even you,' he said flatly.

And with that he turned round and abruptly left the cabin, preferring the darkness and the drizzling rain to any kind of comfort she could offer him.

CHAPTER NINE

JOSIE had to suppress the almost overwhelmingly strong impulse to run after Daniel. Instead, she sank back on to the sleeping-bag, let her aching head rest against her linked hands, and wondered if she was ever going to be the same person again, once this long, long night was finally over.

Probably not, she thought wearily. She felt years older, and weighed down with the weight of everything Daniel had told her. If this was what being in love was like, then she didn't like it. It meant feeling other people's pain as if it were your own. Hurting perhaps even more than they did, because you felt so helpless to do anything about it.

She could hear the rain still pattering down on to the roof of the cabin, and she wondered if Daniel was still walking around in it, or if he had gone to the comparative warmth and comfort of the minibus. She thought he was probably still walking around, his clothes soaked through by now. There was sometimes an odd sort of release in physical discomfort.

After a while, she curled up in a small ball and closed her aching eyes. That didn't shut out the pictures inside her head, though. Her and Daniel lying on this same sleeping-bag, his body hard and hot against hers, but his hands curiously gentle. Perhaps deliberately gentle, because he was a man who had learnt to be afraid of any kind of violence. And the blurred image of a woman who didn't have a name or a face, but who had deliberately destroyed her baby, not only because she valued her career more, but because she derived a sick pleasure from hurting the man who had fathered that child.

Josie shivered. She wasn't violently anti-abortion, although she didn't think that it was something she could ever do herself. She recognised that there were certain circumstances in which a woman might find herself with no other choice, and have to make that painful decision. But she couldn't imagine how anyone could do it in that terrible way, using it as a weapon to inflict pain on someone.

The long hours of the night crawled by with incredible slowness. Once, she got up and looked out into the darkness, but there was no sign of Daniel. The rain had stopped and the sky was clearing. She could see the dim outline of the minibus, but didn't dare go over to see if he was inside. He didn't want her around; he wasn't going to make any kind of place for her in his life. The sooner she got used to that idea, the quicker she was going to recover from all the shocks of tonight.

Except that Josie was quite certain that there were some things that she wasn't ever going to recover from completely. Daniel Hayden had lit something inside her that it was going to be difficult—perhaps even impossible—to put out. How had he done it? she wondered with a fresh rush of confusion. She didn't know, couldn't explain it. She was only sure that it had happened. That damned bolt of lightning, she thought with a touch of bitterness. Derek hadn't warned her that it could turn on you, and be dangerous and destructive.

Dawn finally came, with a glowing brightness that didn't at all match her mood. She hadn't slept, and she felt tired and sluggish. As well as that, her body ached; a queer, unfamiliar ache, that seemed to seep into the very depths of her bones.

She washed with cold water, which should have refreshed her, but didn't. Her gold curls drooped limply, as if to match the way she felt, and there was no colour in her face.

When she finally opened the door of the cabin, she found that Daniel was standing just outside. Seeing him like that made her jump. She had thought that it would be a little while yet before she had to face him.

'I was just coming to see if you were up,' he said briefly.

'Yes, I am,' Josie answered unsteadily. She couldn't seem to stop looking at him. His face was very familiar, but her eyes still fixed on the strong lines of his cheekbones, the high forehead with the swept back golden-brown hair, and the slightly grim set of his mouth. Oh, yes, she was certainly very familiar with his mouth! She could remember *exactly* how it had felt as it moved against hers; how it had created hot trails of pleasure as those flexible lips had explored all the intimate curves of her body, stopping now and then to nuzzle leisurely and at length before moving on to create devastation somewhere else . . .

With a huge effort, she pushed away the pictures and memories. If she went on like this, she was going to drive herself quite mad!

'What are we going to do today?' she asked, somehow managing to keep her voice remarkably steady.

'I think it will be best if we keep to our original plan and drive straight back to Thimphu.' He was looking in her direction, but his eyes seemed to be fixed on a point just beyond her, as if he didn't want to look directly into her own dark blue gaze. 'It's a long drive, but if we start off right now and don't hit any problems we should be there early tonight.'

'I'll go and get my things, then.'

For the first time, the rather blank expression on his face shifted and altered, and his features registered faint surprise.

'You don't mind leaving? And with no questions? No arguments?'

'If I thought it would do any good, I'd argue with you until I ran out of breath,' Josie said in a low tone. 'But you've made up your mind about this, haven't you? Made up your mind about *me*?'

Daniel moved a little restlessly, as if he didn't want to talk about it. 'I said a lot more last night than I ever meant to say,' he muttered at last. 'But perhaps you at least understand a few things rather better now. And you know why I'm not ready for any kind of serious relationship.'

At that, Josie's eyes suddenly flared. 'Then why did you touch me in the first place?' she demanded, her raw nerves adding extra fierceness to her voice. 'Or did you think I was some dumb little blonde that you could play around with for a while, and then dump when you got tired of me?'

His own gaze flickered dangerously. 'I never thought of you in that way. And all right, I'll admit that I've made a lot of mistakes over the last few days. I shouldn't have brought you with me, shouldn't have given in to the need to touch you, shouldn't have let myself——' He abruptly stopped, as if he was once again saying far more than he had ever meant to. When he finally started speaking again, his voice was much flatter and rigidly controlled. 'When we started off on this trip, I didn't ever think that it would end like this. I didn't foresee any of this.'

'Then what *did* you think would happen?' Josie asked angrily. 'Especially once you reached the point where you couldn't keep your hands off me?'

She hadn't meant to say anything like that. She knew this was all going wrong and getting worse with every word they said to each other, but all the pent-up emotions inside her were threatening to burst out, and she didn't seem to have any control over the words that poured out of her.

Daniel's face had grown dark now, as if his own mood was as volatile as her own.

'You didn't seem to mind being touched,' he reminded her. 'You didn't make much effort to stop me.'

'That's because I didn't know that was *all* that you wanted,' Josie flashed back at him. 'I didn't know you were an emotional cripple. That you either don't have any feelings, or you're too damned scared to show them!'

She knew that blow was well below the belt, but she was past the point where she cared. All right, so he had been through a hell of a time because of a bad relationship, but did that give him the right to drag *her* into the mess he had made of his life? Turn her into a victim, as well?

Daniel growled something under his breath. Then he made an obvious effort to hold on to his simmering temper. 'What do you want me to do?' he said curtly. 'Apologise? Fine, I'll do that. I'm sorry I laid a finger on you, sorry I even brought you to Bhutan. But before you put every scrap of blame on me, remember that I warned you what I was like, I explained very clearly that I wasn't looking for any kind of involvement. I really don't think it's my fault if you were stupid enough to fall in love with me.'

'Stupid?' echoed Josie furiously. *'Stupid?'*

He ran his fingers through his hair in an oddly distracted gesture. 'OK, that was a bad choice of word,' he muttered. 'And most of the fault *was* mine. I don't see what I can do about it now, though, except get you back to Calcutta and then get out of your life.'

'I can make my own way back to Calcutta,' Josie insisted at once. After everything that had happened, she really didn't think she could face that long journey with him, all those hours spent in his company. It would be like a very special kind of purgatory. 'I can also get back to Thimphu on my own,' she went on determinedly. 'There must be someone who'll give me a lift.'

'I'm not leaving you here, in the middle of Bhutan,' Daniel said at once. 'If I can't do anything else for you, I can at least make sure you get back home safely.'

'I'll be perfectly all right. You're not responsible for me and there's absolutely no need for you to worry about me. I can look after myself.'

'If you could look after yourself, you'd never have got involved with me,' he said in a flat tone. 'No one with an ounce of sense would ever have done that.'

Josie suddenly swallowed hard. He was right, of course. It didn't make any difference to the way she felt at the moment, though. She just wanted to get away from him. It was the only way she was ever going to get through this.

'I don't need you to take me back to Thimphu,' she insisted again, in a low but stubborn voice. 'Just go, and leave me here.'

Daniel didn't even answer her. Instead, he went into the cabin and came out again a minute later, carrying her things.

'What are you doing?' she demanded suspiciously.

He walked over to the minibus, still without saying another word, and slung her stuff in the back. Then he finally turned to face her.

'I know that I'm probably the last person in the world you want to be with right now,' he said rather grimly, 'but if I leave you here, without knowing if you ever got back home safely, I won't be able to sleep at nights. I probably won't be able to, anyway,' he added, an odd grimace crossing his face. 'But that'll be my problem, not yours.'

'What if I refuse to go?'

'I'll pick you up and throw you inside.' His tone was level, but the dangerous gleam in his eyes warned her that he would do exactly that, if he had to. 'If you don't want to sit in the front, beside me, get in the back. That way, you won't have to talk to me, or even look at me.'

Josie immediately hopped into the back. It was rather cramped, since she was sharing the space with their sleeping-bags, spare clothes and supplies, but at least she was putting as much distance as possible between herself and Daniel.

The long journey that followed was the most miserable that she could ever remember. As the minibus bumped and rattled its way back to Thimphu, there was plenty of time for her anger to fade slowly away, and a lot of other more complicated emotions to take its place. They made just a couple of brief stops, and they didn't say a single word to each other.

By the time they finally rolled into Thimphu, they had been travelling for hours and it was dark. Josie was glad of that. She didn't want Daniel to see her face—it might have revealed too much.

As she climbed stiffly out of the minibus, she found he had parked it outside the hotel where they had stayed before.

'It's late, but you should be able to get a room,' Daniel said shortly.

'You're not staying here?' The words popped out before she could stop them, and she immediately regretted saying them. He might think that she wanted him to stay in the same hotel and she didn't, she definitely didn't, she told herself very fiercely.

'I think it would be better if I stayed somewhere else,' he said, after a brief pause. 'Your plane back to Calcutta leaves in the morning. I'll make sure you've got a seat on it. I'll be staying on in Thimphu for a couple more days. There are more officials I have to see, and red tape to be dealt with.'

'Then we won't see each other again.' She tried to keep her tone as flat and emotionless as his own, but wasn't at all sure that she had succeeded.

'Not for a while, at least. I suppose there's always a chance that we might run into each other at some time in the future.' His voice rather abruptly changed. 'The trouble was that we met at the wrong time. You were on the rebound from someone else, and I still can't seem to break away from the past. Maybe if we give it time, things will be better between us if we ever meet up again.'

With that, he quickly turned away from her, got back into the minibus and drove off.

Josie stood there for a long time after he had gone. Then she finally blinked away the brightness from her eyes and trudged into the hotel.

It had been so long since she had slept that as soon as she reached her room she flopped on to the bed and plunged straight into exhausted unconsciousness. It was a very fitful sleep, though, and riddled with dark, unpleasant dreams.

In the morning, she woke up feeling as if she hadn't slept at all, but she dragged herself out of bed. She had to catch the plane back to Calcutta. And from there she would go home.

What would she do when she was back in England? she wondered wearily. Sit in her small flat, brooding and moping? Go back home to her parents for a while, to be cosseted and cared for, like a small child who couldn't cope with the hefty knocks life handed out? Both of those prospects were totally unappealing. Just get through today, she advised herself in the end. That, in itself, was hard enough. Trying to think any further ahead than that was too much; she couldn't cope with it, not right now.

Right up to the moment when she got on the plane that would take her back to Calcutta, a small part of her thought—hoped, a little desperately—that Daniel would board the plane with her. It was only when they were actually in the air that she had to admit that he had meant every word he had said. He was staying in Bhutan, and she was on the first leg of her long journey back to England—without him.

When she finally got off the plane at Calcutta, the heat hit her like an almost physical blow. After the fresh, sweet air of Bhutan, the humidity seemed to clog her lungs and make it hard to breathe.

Josie knew that she had to try and change her ticket for her flight back to England. Her original ticket had been booked as part of the package tour that had first brought her here. The tour hadn't been due to return until the end of the week. If she wanted to go back to England straight away, she would have to change it for an earlier flight.

Quite suddenly, though, she couldn't face all the hassle involved, the explanations and the forms that would have to be filled in. She would sooner stay in Calcutta for a couple of days, and then go home on the original flight. Anyway, she wasn't in any hurry to go home. In fact, right now she didn't particularly care where she was.

She wandered out of the airport, the humidity bringing her skin out in a light sheen of sweat. She felt lost and alone. India was too big a country for someone on their own to cope with. It was too hot, too crowded, too exotic—Josie began to feel more and more overwhelmed.

A taxi driver screeched to a halt in front of her, sensing a prospective fare. 'I can take you to a good hotel,' the driver offered with a big smile. 'Very cheap, very clean, very reasonable.'

Without really thinking what she was doing, Josie climbed into the taxi. She couldn't wander around the airport all day. The taxi shot off in the direction of Calcutta, and soon it was rattling through the crowded streets, which were just as noisy, vibrant and strong-smelling as she remembered them.

She suddenly leant forward. 'I don't want to go to a hotel,' she told the driver.

He screeched to a halt in the middle of the road, completely ignoring the blaring horns of the cars and trucks that had been forced to stop very suddenly behind him.

'Where would you like to go?' he asked affably.

Josie didn't know. She was just quite certain that she couldn't face a crowded hotel, full of strangers, and set in the middle of these streets packed with people, traffic and animals, relentlessly noisy and overwhelming.

A traffic jam began to build up behind them and the blaring horns got louder. She started to panic. Where *could* she go? Where was it quiet and less crowded, somewhere she could lick her wounds in relative peace?

From out of nowhere, the answer popped into her head. Before she realised what she was doing, she was giving the taxi driver the address of the house where Daniel's aunt Katherine was staying.

He crunched the taxi into gear, veered round a herd of goats, narrowly missed a huge truck hurtling in the opposite direction and then shot off down a side-street.

Josie sat back in her seat and told herself that she would have to tell him to stop. She couldn't possibly turn up on the doorstop of the house where Daniel's aunt was staying. What would she say? What possible kind of explanation could she give for being there?

The taxi rattled on, though, and still she said nothing. Even when he finally pulled up outside the Maharaja's imposing house, she didn't tell him she had changed her mind and he was to drive on. Instead, she got out of the taxi, handed over the fare, and watched rather numbly as he drove away.

She stood outside the large white house for nearly five minutes. Then she picked up her bag, walked up to the front door and rang the bell.

It was Daniel's aunt who opened it, in person. 'I've been watching you from the window, wondering if you were ever going to pluck up the nerve to come in,' she said with a smile. 'I nearly opened the door a couple of times, to ask you, but it looked like a decision that you had to make for yourself.'

Josie didn't say anything. In fact, she didn't know what she *could* say.

His aunt continued to look at her slightly quizzically. 'What are you doing here?' she asked at last.

'I don't know,' Josie muttered miserably.

'Well, you'd better come inside,' she said in a practical tone. 'You took tired and rather ill. Has Daniel been mistreating you? He doesn't usually behave badly with women, but he hasn't been himself lately. He's had—rather a lot of problems.'

'Do you know about them?' asked Josie in a rather croaky voice.

'Not all the details, but I do know he got mixed up with someone who put him through a great deal more than he deserved. Men!' said his aunt, with a touch of exasperation. 'Why do they so often choose women who are completely wrong for them? It's all to do with this complicated business of sex, I suppose. It addles the brains of even the most intelligent of men. Are you hungry?'

The unexpected question, tagged on the end, threw Josie for a moment. With an effort, she made herself answer. 'Not really. I shouldn't even be here, I don't know why I came. I think I'd better go.'

She went to pick up her case, but Daniel's aunt got there first. 'You're here because you need somewhere to stay and you can't face a hotel,' she said firmly. 'And I'm the only person you know in Calcutta. Come on in and I'll find you a room.'

'I really don't think I should,' Josie muttered. 'Anyway, what about the Maharaja? He won't want a stranger staying in his house.'

'The Maharaja's away until next week. And he's a very hospitable and kind man. He won't mind in the least if I invite a friend to stay.'

'I'm not really a friend. You hardly know me.'

'That's very easy to put right,' said Daniel's aunt. 'Move in for a couple of days, and we'll soon get to know each other.'

It was so tempting. The house was so cool and quiet. And this woman was Daniel's aunt. In an odd way, it was almost like being close to him.

'I still think I should go to a hotel,' Josie said, although very half-heartedly.

His aunt was already carrying her case into the house, though. 'You probably want a bath,' she was saying briskly, as if the matter had already been settled. 'And you look very tired. Perhaps you should try and have a sleep before dinner.'

Josie gave in. In fact, she didn't seem to have the strength of will to do anything else. She trotted meekly along behind Daniel's aunt as she led her up to a large airy bedroom, with a magnificent bathroom leading off it. The bath itself was big enough to take half a dozen people comfortably, the gold taps glistened, exquisitely patterned tiles covered the walls and the floor, and there were shelves heaped with soft towels, expensive soaps and scented oils.

'I'll leave you to settle in,' said his aunt. 'Sleep for as long as you like after your bath. If you don't want to get out of bed, you can have your dinner on a tray.'

In fact, Josie nearly fell asleep in the bath. The water was marvellously hot and relaxing, and smelt delicious after she had extravagantly poured in scented oil from one of the bottles on the shelf.

She couldn't quite believe that she was actually here. Or that Daniel's aunt had welcomed her, and not asked any awkward or difficult questions. Josie sleepily told herself that she would leave in the morning. After a restful night, she would feel better and more capable of coping with everything that had happened.

In the morning, though, she didn't want to get out of bed. She didn't feel ill or feverish. She just didn't want to get up. Daniel's aunt didn't seem to mind. She didn't even lecture Josie when she couldn't eat the small delicacies that were meant to tempt her non-existent appetite.

'I've been like this a couple of times,' she told Josie briskly. 'It's as if your mind and body need to close down for a couple of days, and do absolutely nothing until they've had a chance to rest and get themselves back into some kind of order.'

'I'm putting you to a lot of trouble,' mumbled Josie.

'I like a little trouble now and then,' said his aunt cheerfully. 'It's been rather boring here since the Maharaja went away. Anyway, I feel sort of responsible for you. I'm the one who told you that you'd be safe with Daniel. I should have realised that my nephew's the type of man that no woman's really safe with.'

Josie closed her eyes. She didn't want to talk about Daniel. She didn't even want to think about him. His aunt quickly got the message and tactfully withdrew. Josie slept for a while and woke up again feeling very slightly hungry. The hot ache behind her eyes wasn't quite so bad, and she felt the first stirrings of life creeping back into her.

By the next morning, she was out of bed and eating normally. Daniel's aunt watched with some satisfaction as she ate her way through a huge breakfast.

'At least you're not going to fade away before my eyes,' she said. 'I'm going shopping this morning. Do you want to come with me?'

But Josie definitely didn't feel capable yet of coping with the noisy, crowded confusion of Calcutta's streets.

'I'd rather stay here—if you don't mind?'

'I don't mind in the least,' said his aunt. 'Do whatever you like. I'll probably be back for lunch, so I'll see you then.'

After she had gone, the large house seemed very empty. Josie knew that the Maharaja employed quite a few staff, but they moved around quietly and discreetly, and she rarely saw them. She wandered around the empty rooms for a while, and then went out into the garden.

The sun shone down hotly, and brilliantly coloured flowers cascaded out of pots and trailed over walls. The bright glare dazzled her for a few moments, after the shaded coolness of the house. Her eyes slowly adjusted to the brightness, and it was then that she saw the tall figure standing in the open doorway that led from the house to the garden.

Daniel Hayden looked as shocked to see her as she was to see him. He took a couple of steps forward and then stopped, the sun beating down on his head and striking vivid gold glints in his hair. They stared at each other for a long, long time. Then Daniel came a little nearer.

'I never expected to find you here,' he said abruptly.

'I never meant to *come* here,' Josie said shakily. 'I just sort of ended up on your aunt's doorstep. I'm not sure how it happened.'

'And my aunt, being the sort of person she is, took you in.'

'She's certainly looked after me very well for the last couple of days.'

'Looked after you?' Daniel repeated sharply. 'Have you been ill?'

Josie gave a rather confused shake of her head. It was so hard to think straight, with him standing there only a few yards away. 'No, not ill. I just felt—not quite right.'

'And I suppose that was my fault.' His tone was slightly harsh now.

'It wasn't anyone's fault,' she said rather tiredly. 'And I'm sorry I came here. I didn't mean to—and I didn't come because I was trying to see you again. I didn't know you'd be calling in to see your aunt. I'll pack my things and leave.'

'Where will you go?'

'That doesn't really bother you, does it? As long as you get rid of me?' There was a faint note of bitterness in her voice and she knew, from the shadow that crossed his face, that he had heard it.

'I've missed you,' he said abruptly.

'We've only been apart for a couple of days.'

'It's seemed a lot longer than that. I suppose I've got used to having you around.'

'A week and a half ago, you didn't even know me,' Josie reminded him.

For the first time, a ghost of a smile touched the corners of his mouth. 'A week and a half ago, I seemed like a rather different person.'

Her dark blue eyes opened a little wider. 'Are you saying that I changed you?'

'I'm not sure what you've done to me.' Daniel took a couple of rather restless paces forward, and Josie's nerves twitched.

'I don't want you to come any nearer,' she said edgily.

He stood very still again, and looked at her. 'I've said a lot of things to you that I wish I hadn't said. Things which I meant at the time, but are now beginning to seem like a lot of nonsense.'

'Back in Bhutan, you were fairly certain that you didn't want to see me again. At least, not for a long time.'

He gave a faint grimace. 'These last couple of days have seemed like a long time! And I knew that I'd missed you, but I didn't realise quite how much until I walked into the garden and saw you standing there.'

Josie stared at him, every nerve in her body raw and aching. 'Why are you saying all these things to me? People don't change overnight. And when we were in Bhutan all you seemed to want to do was to get away from me.'

'Everyone makes mistakes.' He gave another faint grin. 'Even me. And I'm amazed at the way I've missed you arguing with me and yelling at me.'

'I didn't yell at you,' Josie denied indignantly. 'At least, not very often,' she rather hurriedly amended, as she remembered one or two occasions when her voice had definitely been rather louder than usual. 'Anyway, the way I shouted at you wasn't a problem. The *real* problem was that you were scared to get involved. You made all sorts of excuses, telling me that I was still on the rebound from Derek, and that you weren't interested in relationships, but when it came down to it you were simply frightened to feel anything for me.'

'It still scares the hell out of me,' Daniel admitted. 'But once you'd left Bhutan and I was on my own again I soon began to realise that I didn't like that, either. I didn't like it at all. I decided that I didn't want to wait and see if we ran into each other again by chance, at some time in the future. I wanted to head straight back to England, to tell you that I'd made some very large and serious mistakes. I was going to catch the plane this afternoon, after I'd called in to see Aunt Katherine.'

'Oh,' said Josie, in a rather small voice.

'Finding you here was a pretty hefty surprise. But the kind of surprise I'd like to get more often,' he said a little huskily.

'Oh,' she said again, having some trouble getting out anything except the very shortest and simplest of words.

'I can't really promise you anything,' Daniel went on. 'I don't know how this is going to work out. There are still problems we'll have to work through, and others that we haven't even faced yet. I don't suppose that any of it's going to be very easy, but you seem a girl who can cope with most things—including me. If you want to try, of course.'

'Yes, I want to try,' she said rather breathlessly, and without the slightest hesitation. Then her eyes clouded over again. 'You do really mean all of this?' she said in an uncertain voice. 'You won't suddenly change your mind again and walk out?'

'I'm not going anywhere unless you come with me,' he assured her steadily. 'If I throw away this chance, what is the rest of my life going to be like? Empty and meaningless. All work and no real closeness to anyone—no love. But together I think we can pull each other through any bad patches that still lie ahead, and come out of this with something that's good and lasting.' His gold gaze looked straight at her. 'Do you think we can make it, Josie?'

'Yes,' she said softly.

'Good.' His smile was much wider this time. 'Then why don't you come inside, and I can kiss you without all the servants peering at us out of the windows?'

Josie followed him into the coolness of the house, her heart thumping away so hard that she thought everyone within a hundred yards must be able to hear it. I don't believe this is happening, she told herself several times. I simply don't believe it!

But the warm, hard pressure of Daniel's mouth just seconds after they had stepped inside the house finally convinced her. The kiss went on and on until they were both breathless, hot and shaking. Daniel pulled her down on to a nearby sofa. He swung her legs up, lay down beside her, and then slid open her thin cotton blouse as if the softness of her breasts was the one thing in this world that he craved.

For just a moment, a shadow of doubt crossed Josie's face. Was this all that he really wanted from her? This physical closeness, the warm, sweet pleasure that her body could give him?

As if he could read her mind, Daniel raised his head and his gold-brown eyes gleamed down at her. 'This is very good, but it isn't everything,' he said softly. 'If I wanted just this, I could get it from any willing woman. But I want more. If you stick around, you'll find out just how much more I want—need—from you.'

Josie looked up at him. 'I still can't quite believe you're saying all these things. Not after everything that happened back in Bhutan.'

'I told you, I've changed. No, I haven't changed,' he corrected himself. '*You've* changed me. I haven't the slightest idea how you've done it, only that it's happened.'

'You don't mind any more that I love you?' she asked, a hint of timidness creeping back into her voice.

'I'd mind like hell if you didn't,' Daniel replied roughly. He bent his head again and his mouth caressed the softness of her breasts and licked the small hard peaks. Then he took one more fierce kiss from her. 'I don't know what you've done to me,' he groaned, 'but I don't think I'm ever going to recover from it!'

Josie gave a small sigh of satisfaction. At the same time, her hands moved over him with loving possessiveness.

He stood it for as long as he could. Then he took a deep shuddering breath and pulled away from her. 'I think you'd better stop—and right now!'

'Why?' she asked, with an innocent smile.

'Because Aunt Katherine might return at any moment, and, if she does, I don't want to be in the middle of something that would shock my favourite maiden aunt!'

'Your aunt doesn't strike me as being particularly strait-laced or shockable.'

'She isn't, but she does have very high moral standards. For example,' went on Daniel, 'if things work out between us—and I think they might, I really think they might—she'll almost certainly force me to marry you.'

Josie's eyes grew very wide. 'Marry me?' Then a touch of the old wariness returned to her face. 'Are you ready for that kind of commitment yet?'

'I've no idea,' he replied truthfully. 'But I've the feeling that you'll help me to cope with it.'

'Would you really have to be forced into it?'

'If we carry on like this,' Daniel said, his voice rather muffled now as his mouth nuzzled against the warm swell of her breast, 'then no one is going to have to use any force at all. In fact, *I'll* probably be the one dragging *you* down the aisle.'

The distant sound of a door opening and then closing again made both of them suddenly jump. 'Oh, hell,' muttered Daniel. 'Aunt Katherine!'

He abandoned her breasts with regret, swiftly re-fastened her blouse, and then ran his fingers through his own dishevelled hair.

'Do we look as if we've been doing anything too disrespectable?' he said with a quick grin.

'We don't look it,' said Josie. 'But I certainly *feel* it.'

'Good,' he said with some satisfaction. 'I intend to make you feel like that for most of the time, in the future.'

And with that slightly alarming, yet very pleasurable promise of Daniel's whirling round inside her head, Josie slid her hand through his and, with her dark blue eyes glowing, went with him to meet his aunt.

OFFICIAL RULES • MILLION DOLLAR BIG WIN SWEEPSTAKES
NO PURCHASE OR OBLIGATION NECESSARY TO ENTER

To enter, follow the directions published. **ALTERNATE MEANS OF ENTRY:** Hand-print your name and address on a 3″×5″ card and mail to either: Harlequin Big Win, 3010 Walden Ave., P.O. Box 1867, Buffalo, NY 14269-1867, or Harlequin Big Win, P.O. Box 609, Fort Erie, Ontario L2A 5X3, and we will assign your Sweepstakes numbers (Limit: one entry per envelope). For eligibility, entries must be received no later than March 31, 1994 and be sent via 1st-class mail. No liability is assumed for printing errors or lost, late or misdirected entries.

To determine winners, the sweepstakes numbers on submitted entries will be compared against a list of randomly preselected prizewinning numbers. In the event all prizes are not claimed via the return of prizewinning numbers, random drawings will be held from among all other entries received to award unclaimed prizes.

Prizewinners will be determined no later than May 30, 1994. Selection of winning numbers and random drawings are under the supervision of D.L. Blair, Inc., an independent judging organization whose decisions are final. One prize to a family or organization. No substitution will be made for any prize, except as offered. Taxes and duties on all prizes are the sole responsibility of winners. Winners will be notified by mail. Chances of winning are determined by the number of entries distributed and received.

Sweepstakes open to persons 18 years of age or older, except employees and immediate family members of Torstar Corporation, D.L. Blair, Inc., their affiliates, subsidiaries and all other agencies, entities and persons connected with the use, marketing or conduct of this Sweepstakes. All applicable laws and regulations apply. Sweepstakes offer void wherever prohibited by law. Any litigation within the province of Quebec respecting the conduct and awarding of a prize in this Sweepstakes must be submitted to the Régies des Loteries et Courses du Quebec. In order to win a prize, residents of Canada will be required to correctly answer a time-limited arithmetical skill-testing question. Values of all prizes are in U.S. currency.

Winners of major prizes will be obligated to sign and return an affidavit of eligibility and release of liability within 30 days of notification. In the event of non-compliance within this time period, prize may be awarded to an alternate winner. Any prize or prize notification returned as undeliverable will result in the awarding of the prize to an alternate winner. By acceptance of their prize, winners consent to use of their names, photographs or other likenesses for purposes of advertising, trade and promotion on behalf of Torstar Corporation without further compensation, unless prohibited by law.

This Sweepstakes is presented by Torstar Corporation, its subsidiaries and affiliates in conjunction with book, merchandise and/or product offerings. Prizes are as follows: Grand Prize—$1,000,000 (payable at $33,333.33 a year for 30 years). First through Sixth Prizes may be presented in different creative executions, each with the following approximate values: First Prize—$35,000; Second Prize—$10,000; 2 Third Prizes—$5,000 each; 5 Fourth Prizes—$1,000 each; 10 Fifth Prizes—$250 each; 1,000 Sixth Prizes—$100 each. Prizewinners will have the opportunity of selecting any prize offered for that level. A travel-prize option if offered and selected by winner, must be completed within 12 months of selection and is subject to hotel and flight accommodations availability. Torstar Corporation may present this sweepstakes utilizing names other than Million Dollar Sweepstakes. For a current list of all prize options offered within prize levels and all names the Sweepstakes may utilize, send a self-addressed stamped envelope (WA residents need not affix return postage) to: Million Dollar Sweepstakes Prize Options/Names, P.O. Box 7410, Blair, NE 68009.

For a list of prizewinners (available after July 31, 1994) send a separate, stamped self-addressed envelope to: Million Dollar Sweepstakes Winners, P.O. Box 4728, Blair NE 68009.

SWP193

HARLEQUIN PRESENTS®

A Year
DOWN UNDER

In February, we will take you to Sydney, Australia, with
NO GENTLE SEDUCTION by Helen Bianchin,
Harlequin Presents #1527.

Lexi Harrison and Georg Nicolaos move in the right
circles. Lexi's a model and Georg is a wealthy Sydney
businessman. Life seems perfect . . . so why have they
agreed to a *pretend* engagement?

Share the adventure—and the romance—
of A Year Down Under!

Available this month in
A YEAR DOWN UNDER

HEART OF THE OUTBACK
by Emma Darcy
Harlequin Presents #1519
Wherever Harlequin books are sold.   YDU-J